Turl Street Tales

Our thanks to Sara Banerji,
for her patience, perspicacity
– and jam tarts.

Credits

While many of the places and people mentioned in these tales are real, the scenarios are the product of the authors' delusions.

- Photos of Turl Street in Oxford and the QI Club (now the Corner Club) by Nicola Wilcox
- Photo of a gargoyle from Turl Street by Isabel James
- Map by Liz Henderson

All profits will be shared with
Maggie's Cancer Information Centre, Oxford
www.maggiescentres.org

Turl Street Tales

The Turl Street Writers

Published 2008 by arima publishing

www.arimapublishing.com

ISBN 978 1 84549 349 3

© Contributors 2008

Printed and bound in the United Kingdom

Typeset in Garamond 11/14

Swirl is an imprint of arima publishing.

arima publishing
ASK House, Northgate Avenue
Bury St Edmunds, Suffolk IP32 6BB
t: (+44) 01284 700321
www.arimapublishing.com

Contents

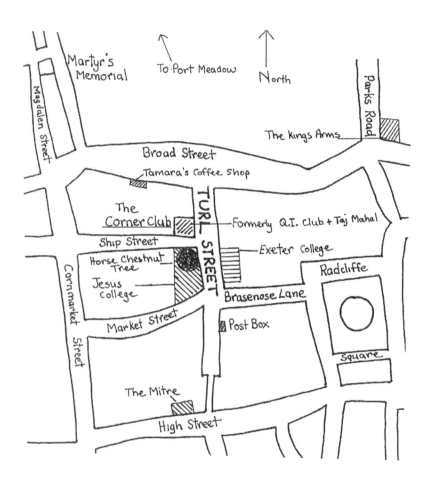

Map of Oxford

The QI Club, 16 Turl Street, Oxford

Quite An Inspiring Corner - 16 Turl Street
Penny MacLeod

It's a friendly building. And a convivial one. If a building contained some sort of electro-magnetic memory of the people who had inhabited it, then this building – for so many years housing the Taj Mahal Indian restaurant – must have soaked up the imprint of thousands of convivial meals where people enjoyed each other's company. It must also have been infused with the exoticism of the spices in the dishes that cheered the spirits of the post-war students when the Bahadur brothers set up business in 1945 – the first Indian restaurant in Britain.

Before its incarnation as a restaurant, the building probably was used as commercial premises, but going back to 1820 the Ship Street side of the building was a coffee-house: a place to gossip and share information and feel sophisticated. And that is what this building invites us to do. The rooms are cosy in the winter – the lounge upstairs has an open fire where Robin dried his socks arriving soaked at our meeting after cycling in the pouring rain from Headington. But we usually meet in the green library on the top floor. This room incubates inspiration – the pieces we write there flow and amuse us. Yvonne reads us her diary of an Oxford Don's wife (some of it written 20 or 30 years ago), dropping papers on the floor and complaining at her own disorganisation. We implore her to put the whole lot in an envelope and send it off to several agents. The room doesn't mind – she has captured the richness of life in this cerebral city. Publishing be damned.

This building loves laughter and vivacity. It was built in 1785 by Mr Priddy to house some of the scholars of Exeter College who must have cut many a caper – climbing in through windows after curfew, and ruining their eyesight by writing by candlelight at 2 am during their essay crises. What escapades and amorous encounters did they recount here – and earnest intellectual discussions did they hold?

Sitting at the round table in the library Sara Banerji gives us five minutes to write a character sketch. Our life experiences provide them: Julia's tale of the young man from Chechnya whose jaw clenches when he spits out the name of his native country; my tale of the Cuban rap artist whom my student daughter married and who now dances round my kitchen and raps when I play a Salsa track. Sara's anecdotes of running away from her family in Rhodesia and tea planting in India demonstrate that "everything is copy".

We absorb and reflect the personalities of the numerous people we meet in our lives – and so does this building on the corner of Ship and Turl Streets. Sarah Lloyd, Manager of the QI Club, describes it as a meeting place for all the tribes of Oxford. Dentists, academics, students, writers and dancers – all find refuge and refreshment here. Want to bump into an astrophysicist without going to a laboratory, or overhear a beautician waxing lyrical? This is the place. It is a coffee house for our times and it thrives on the caffeine of inspiration. Some writers still hand-write their books here; Sara Banerji hosts literary lunches; comedy sketches are written over an exotic vodka in the cellar Bar. Ted Dewan, a North Oxford artist, constructed a pendulum in the Panelled Club Room for the spire centrepiece of the Luminox fire show; and also held his pyrotechnics planning meetings there. Jazz musicians such as Chyna perform in the Bar after dark. All these creative endeavours give back to the building the inspiration that it holds within its walls – like compound interest, it multiplies.

John Lloyd (producer of *Not the Nine O'Clock News*, *Spitting Image* and *Blackadder*) and John Mitchinson, publishing impresario, conceived and founded the *QI* television programme. Together they had discovered a passion for interesting things not generally available, and so assembled a team of people to research the programme (now in series 'E'). The researchers originally worked at the top of the Turl Street building. What to do with the floors below? Provide meeting rooms for a club with an eclectic membership, of course. And then add a bar and bookshop open to the public. Not just a place to socialise, people could walk in off the street and find a book to make their lives, and themselves, more interesting.

Whether a member of the public or a member of the club, the best thing about this incarnation of the building is that people who otherwise wouldn't have met, have spoken to each other within these walls and exchanged ideas.

We order lunch after a meeting and Charlie the waitress takes thirteen orders without writing anything down. Ten minutes later she places each person's order in front of them without having to check which dish they ordered. With bohemian authority, she remembers the drinks orders, too. She's that sort of girl. It's that sort of place.

The Writing Group
Val Watkins

Every Wednesday, about ten thirty in the morning, The Turl Street Writers climbed the old wooden staircase of the QI Club to the library. Seven or eight of them would sit at an old round table to discuss their latest contributions for the next publication.

The QI Club was a tall, narrow building in Oxford on the corner of Turl Street and Ship Street. As the writers exchanged greetings and settled down, footsteps could be heard clumping on the staircase as the waiters delivered orders of cups of cappuccino, pots of aromatic teas, exotic fruit smoothies and bottles of water.

It was a lovely warm day in June. As the members of the group started to read their latest pieces Oxford carried on its busy routine. Through the open window they could hear delivery lorries, beeping horns and people shouting. Footsteps ran up and down the staircase, knives and forks rattled as tables were prepared in the dining areas for lunch.

The writers were putting together a book of short stories about the QI Club. They had settled down and were listening to Dora Hartley's piece about the time her aunt's Alsatian got stuck in the catflap. More footsteps were heard coming nearer to the writers' sanctum.

"I'm so sorry I'm late!"

Maisie Burton, a red-faced, bustling woman, burst through the arch into the library. Chairs were shuffled amidst cries of "Never mind" and "There's room here."

"My husband's car wouldn't start and I had to give him a lift to his office and it's totally in the wrong direction for me coming here, and then I had to call in quickly at 'Past Times' for some Victorian postcards ..."

"We were just listening to Dora's latest writing, Maisie," said Amelia Norton, the group's tutor and mentor. "Could you start again, please, Dora? I'm sure the others wouldn't mind hearing that bit again."

Dora was sitting with her lips pursed. She seemed edgy and gave an exaggerated sigh.

" *'We shall have to call the RSPCA. The poor thing's getting strangled.'*
'Easy now, someone call the fire brigade. Give him some air...'
As the fire engine disappeared into the distance Timmy the Alsatian eagerly lapped up a bowl of milk and some biscuits and sat smacking his lips as if nothing had happened. "

"Well," said Amelia, "I think you got the panic of the situation very well there. And it all gets very sensuous. The bit where the head fireman falls passionately in love with your aunt is a real *tour de force*. And what a coincidence he was a member of the QI Club! Do you think you could expand it into a novel?"

"Oh … er … no. I don't think I could, but actually…" said Dora.

"Well, I thought in some parts it was a bit hackneyed," Maisie interrupted, still out of breath. "You used quite a lot of clichés. You made it sound a bit like Mills and Boon."

"I tend to agree with that," Gerald Wilkins added. "It's all a bit contrived and sentimental."

Dora's face flushed bright red.

"Well, that was not intended," she said. "I have written other stories like that. In fact …"

"Let's hear your piece, Maisie," said Amelia.

"Well, I'm afraid I haven't managed to finish my story yet," stuttered Maisie. "I've had so much on this week, what with the school fete and all that …"

"Have you had any ideas?" asked Amelia.

"Erm … I thought I could write about a millionaire who gambles away all his money in the casino, loses his memory and then wins the lottery and marries a princess, but I haven't managed to put anything down yet. I'll have to be careful and not let it get too sentimental."

"And what have you got for us, Gerald?" asked Amelia.

"I've finished my story about the QI Club." Gerald took out his fastidiously neat folder and extracted a very professional-looking sheaf of meticulously typed notes. "It's all ready to add to the full manuscript."

"Could we hear it, then?"

"Do you want me to read all of it?"

"Oh, yes, of course!"

Gerald started to read,

" *The Lost Relics of the Pyramids.* '

The plane pulled away slowly from the deserted runway into the mysterious, vast inky blackness of the midnight sky. The passengers relaxed visibly and turned on their reading lights, or tilted their seats back ready to sleep through the long interminable hours … ' "

A quarter of an hour later Gerald finished reading and sat back satisfied and elated.

"Why don't you bring in a lot more detail about the mummy's tomb?" asked Amelia. "It all fizzled out when you got to that bit. And I expected a lot more mystery about the two Egyptians who were hanging around whispering."

"But I thought that was self-explanatory." Gerald pushed his sheaf of papers petulantly into his folder. "You always tell us to be as economical as we can in short stories and to avoid sentimentality," he said, glancing at Dora.

"It was rather a long short story," muttered Maisie. "How many pages will it take up? And you didn't say much about the QI Club. Still I don't suppose they would have a QI Club in Egypt."

Gerald did not deign to answer.

"How's your novel coming along, Bernard?" asked Amelia.

"Well, I've neglected it a bit as I've been writing my story about the QI Club," said Bernard Wright, shuffling through a lot of random papers and finally selecting two or three of different colours and sizes.

"I've cracked it, though, and I'll get it finished for next week. It's about a sexy young secretary who is madly in love with her unmarried boss. He doesn't seem to notice her, though, and she starts trying out various ruses to attract his attention. I can bring the QI Club into that quite easily."

Bernard looked meaningfully at Maisie who just shrugged her shoulders.

"As for my novel, '*Stand Up the Real Mrs Wotherspoon*', I don't want to divulge any of the plot as I want to get it published somehow. So I'd like it to be a *fait accompli* when you read it. I hope you will find it a real mystery."

It was twelve thirty. The writers began to pack their notebooks and folders away. Maisie was stuffing her folder into a small shopping bag full of packages and toys.

"I really must get myself organised this week and finish my story. No doubt you will have a new story for us next week, Dora. Another of your Mills and Boon masterpieces!" she teased.

The other writers went quiet. Dora, her cheeks red and her eyes bright, looked around at them all.

"Actually, I've been wanting to tell you. I have just this morning received an advance payment for one of my stories from – would you believe – Mills and Boon!"

Street Life
M.S. Clary

Sometimes I wonder how long I've been here. It must be a good fifty years. Maybe more. Time is no longer an issue of any great consequence to me. Some of us have been here for centuries, but I don't have much dealings with them. Disappointed lovers, those seeking revenge. I have no time for that sort of thing.

Perhaps it surprises you to hear that I don't know exactly how long I have been here. You would imagine that the day of my passing would be something I could never forget. Maybe for some it is. But it is more the manner of my leaving that stays with me. I seem to be looking for something. That's why I spend so much time walking up and down these stairs, passing through doors that weren't here in my time and some, like that one on the landing, that once were but are no longer. That is a trick that always gives a passing waitress a start. On occasion, I have to confess, I have done it deliberately. Once or twice a tray has been dropped. It helps time pass. Well, haunting can be very tedious.

Yes, time, that's what I was trying to tell you. It is irretrievably linked to memory and that is the greatest problem for me now. My brain is shot. The nerves and synapses weave and dart, but seldom link. Occasionally there is a brief, wondrous connection, so startling that I feel myself to be on the verge of a complete revelation. But as soon as it comes it fails again, like an electrical wire with a frazzled end.

Sometimes I think I hear my dog, Purcell. Oh yes, he used to come in and sit under my chair. Not the sort of thing they allow nowadays, except in France and Italy, I believe. Not that I ever went to either, but I do hear things said. One of the greatest joys is to listen in to a good conversation. There's not much of that sort of stuff where I come from.

Purcell used to love a strong curry. He would sit patiently while I savoured the delights of a good Rogan Josh. You see, our palates were exhausted from bland wartime food. The *Taj Mahal* offered us the 'Exoticism of the Orient' – that's how the advertisement put it, not quite accurately as I see it now. At the end of the meal, the waiter, Jeremy I used to call him, would put a few scraps into a brown paper bag, and hand them to me as I paid the bill. I think it cost half a crown for a great bowl of steaming meat and rice. I often think of Jeremy. He was good to me and Purcell. I've got it into my head that Jeremy can help me. If only I can remember what help it is I need.

I have tried calling out to him. Jeremy. 'Je-re-m-ee-y' I call, usually at night, when it's quiet, or in the early morning when there are not many people about. But it seems to cause a bit of trouble. There's a bookshop now where the restaurant used to be and a young man with glasses is usually behind the counter. I've tried calling out softly, not wanting to startle him, but this morning he obviously heard something. He became quite upset and went home early. How was I to know that his name was Jeremy?

*

I had to cover for Jeremy today. Had one of his bad heads, he said. When I phoned to find out how he was feeling, he told me he was hearing voices. Asked me if I thought he should see the doctor.

It's lovely and quiet in the bookshop. Not many people know it's here. It's very light too, specially when the sun comes in through the windows. And its shape is round, not like any other. I'm not asked because I know much about books. It's because I've had special training on the tills. Anyway, I prefer it to working in the bar.

I'm a bit worried about Jeremy. This is an old building, lots of history, they say. One of the waitresses had a funny experience upstairs. Said she thought somebody was touching her bottom. But she is a bit highly strung. When she dropped her tray for the second time, she said she saw somebody walking towards her through a wall. Well, that was obviously just an excuse for carelessness.

Another thing I like about the bookshop is that I get to go home earlier than when I'm working in the bar. I shouldn't say this, but I'm going to see if I can take a couple of books out of here tonight. Not to keep, but just to look at when I go home. Some of the pictures in the travel books make me sad for my homeland.

There's a small dog been hanging about here. I've chased him out a couple of times, but I saw him again this morning. If one of the waiters is giving him food, there'll be trouble. I might go to see Jeremy later and find out how he's feeling. I hope he's not cracking up. I'll ask him what the voices said. Maybe they told him we're all due for a rise.

*

"Jeremy, can I come up? I thought you might be hungry. I've brought you a sandwich."

"Carola ?"

"How are you feeling?"

"Much better. I've been in bed all day with an aspirin."

"What about the voices?"

"Thank God they've gone. I must have imagined it."

"What did they say?"

"I'd rather forget about it."

"You can tell me."

"I feel really stupid now."

"Oh, go on."

"Well, it was just a man's voice, calling my name. 'Jeremy', he kept saying. At first I thought it was a customer."

"How can you be sure it wasn't?"

"I was the only person there."

"Are you sure?"

"Well, actually at first I thought it must be that bloke who always comes in first thing and asks for books we haven't got."

"Oh, you mean the one who fancies you."

"Do you really think he does?"

"Does David Beckham play football?"

"Well, I don't think he knows my name."

"So, did the voice say anything else?"

"No, that's what's so strange. Anyway, enough of all that. Were you busy today?"

"Not so bad. Will I see you tomorrow?"

"I hope so. Tell Carl he makes a great sandwich."

*

That day off yesterday seemed to set me up. Carola does a good job when she stands in, but her heart isn't always in it. I think she's homesick for the lakes of Slovenia.

I tidied under the counter, dusted the shelves, checked the till and looked behind the speakers. Nobody hiding here, no funny voices, no … spooks. The morning went well until Dr Zyakowski came in looking for, well, '*A Photographic Jaunt round the Lakes of Slovenia*', actually. I knew we had a copy and I searched everywhere, but couldn't find it. Had to tell him I'd order it for him. Funny thing is the computer lists it as being available. It must have got put back in the wrong section. I'll ask Carola later. Frankly I never know why she's so keen to work in the bookshop. There are more tips in the restaurant.

I found the *'Photographic Jaunt'* later, next to *'Landmarks in the Life of Stalin'* I telephoned Dr Zyakowski and he came in, but wouldn't buy it because some of the photographs were missing. So I've got to order another copy anyway.

*

I thought I might go for a little stroll today. A short walk down Turl Street and into the Broad. There was a time when I was a well-known figure in Blackwells but nobody notices me now.

I expect you will be surprised to learn I frequent the streets and bookstores. We don't just clank along the castle walls in chains you know. No, we can be found anywhere. Railway stations, hospitals, allotments. It's the drama, you see. Those Unforgettable Events. I just wish I could remember what they were.

I overtaxed myself this morning. The wind nearly blew me under a bus. I think I will settle down in one of those nice armchairs upstairs. I still appreciate a bit of comfort. There's that odd group who meet in the library every week. Reading stories they've written, bits of poetry and singing the occasional song. I find it most soothing. Oh, yes, I nearly forgot to tell you – I saw Purcell today. I called out to him, and he looked round and wagged his tail. Maybe I have been barking up the wrong tree.

*

I put them up with Blu Tack and after I'd had my supper – bread with cold sausage and tomato that Carl had slipped me – I put on my pyjamas and lay down on the bed looking at the pictures. The lakes are so beautiful – one was taken on a winter day. It is snowing, and the sky is heavy with dark blue cloud. But the one I like best is where the sun is shining on the water. It reminds me of the summer holidays I used to spend with my grandmother. We would make a picnic, then go for a walk along the lakeside. The fields would be covered in daisies. It rains a lot here, and there is much traffic. Everything costs a great deal of money. I know I shall never see her again, and I sometimes wonder when I will see my home again.

*

"Did you hear anything?"

"No. Is it the voice again?"

"I'm not sure. It's gone so faint."

"Well, that's good, isn't it?"

"Listen. Can you hear anything now?"

"Once back home in Slovenia my grandmother thought she heard noises in the night."

"And was there anyone there?"

"Oh, yes, a bandit had broken into the house and was trying to steal her money. He didn't get anything though, because she shot him."

"What, like dead?"

"Of course. She was a very good shot."

"And did she get arrested?"

"Arrested, for shooting a bandit in her house?"

"Well, that's what could happen here."

"Sometimes, I think this is a very strange country."

"Why did you come here, Carola?"

"Well, after University I wanted to travel. I thought there would be more opportunity."

"Hmm. What did you study?"

"The Psychology of the Paranormal."

"Ah. Well, I've done a thorough check on the books this afternoon. Everything listed is on the shelves, and it's all in the right place."

"You work hard, Jeremy."

"What about a drink tonight, after work?"

"Yes, I'd like that. I'm off at six."

"Same here."

"Have the voices stopped yet, Jeremy?"

"Yes. I think they have."

A Rainy Day
Neil Hancox

The Reverend Robert Edwards pushed tired hair away from his face and adjusted his glasses in an attempt to make sense of the railway timetable he was studying. The interminable rain attacked the rectory windows with malice as if it wanted to get into the kitchen and enjoy the warmth and comfort. Pickles, the aged family cat, nuzzled at his master's feet in the hope of a reward later on. Robert Edwards' fingers tracked down columns and across rows until at last they reached a conclusion.

"It takes nearly two hours to go from Southampton to Oxford by train, with a change in between," he observed to his wife Martha.

She nodded from behind the paper.

"I think," he continued, "that the function of the railways is similar to my own – getting man to his ultimate destination. The journey can take a long time, we are often delayed and we have to wait around in some most unpleasant places."

Martha gave up her battle with today's news.

"A nice one, Bob, but not original you know. It was the Reverend W Awdry of 'Thomas the Tank Engine' fame, who said that. Why don't you have some breakfast?" she added.

He carefully removed the fat from the bacon and fed it to the importuning Pickles who always seemed hungry. Finally the Reverend Edwards swallowed a small pile of pills designed, he trusted, to make this stage of his journey as pleasant as possible.

"What will you be doing in Oxford?" Martha enquired.

"I'm going to the diocesan conference. We are discussing challenges to the church in 2010."

His wife flicked at a crumb of buttery toast adhering to her upper lip with her serviette. That'll keep you busy." Her voice was ecclesiastically even. "Tomorrow I'll be helping at both ends of the spectrum," she said. "Mothers and toddlers and then the aged having a fun time with tea and cake. They can both be very messy."

Robert admired her businesslike approach to life and death and everything in between. She took it as it came. A bit like 'The Charge of the Light Brigade', he had always thought. It was so unlike his own agonising. To do or not to do? Perhaps life was a sandwich, with 'hatch and dispatch', which come to us all, as the bread. His particular problem was what to use for a filling.

The rain continued to drum on the window with an hypnotic rock beat. Inside Pickles, temporarily full, was now asleep on a kitchen chair.

"Are you going to sit there all day, my dear? I've work to do, and I expect you have too. You could start by finding out why our patio is flooding. You know how Pickles hates getting his paws wet." With these encouraging words Martha propelled her husband from the ease of their kitchen into the unknown.

The following day the Reverend Edwards navigated the railway system with surprising ease. The conference was, as such conferences usually were, rather boring but it had a generous lunch break. Instead of engaging in earnest conversations with his fellow clergy over cups of murky coffee, Robert decided to visit a café in The Turl. One of his more adventurous colleagues had described these as offering 'Culture complemented with the drinks and pretty waitresses, weather permitting'. Although a personal representative of the Almighty he could, he believed, enjoy the former and admire the latter.

The sun had fought the rain and won a brief reprieve for Oxford's visitors. While sipping his cappuccino, pleasantly strong and liberally dusted with powdered chocolate, and served by a charming brunette with a heart-lifting bronzed gap between top and bottom of her somewhat skimpy uniform, he read an alarming article on global warming, climate change and carbon footprints. He was familiar with the underlying cause. Greed was a perennial human trait on which he had preached many times, recently pointing out how we were raping the earth with our excessive consumption. The congregation didn't seem unduly moved and one elderly lady had taken him aside and complained about his most unsuitable language. He never seemed able to hit the right note. He was the Reverend Edwards, not the Father-Bob-type-of-vicar.

Today's article was written in apocalyptic journalese. The end was nigher than the occasional placard holder in Cornmarket might have expected. We wouldn't fry or freeze; the deluge would get us. He considered the statement for a minute or so. How very Biblical. That was it! The Flood.

The remainder of the conference was an interference with his new found role, but one that had to be tolerated. His colleagues found him both tending to the hyperactive and more inattentive than usual, a condition they ascribed to overwork and age.

Robert himself was oblivious to such concerns. He had a mission at last, a real mission. He quizzed the fundamentalist sitting next to him about the modern equivalent of a cubit and when the man showed a complete disinterest in boat building repaired to the engineering section of one of the leading Oxford bookshops. The volumes appeared far too technical until he unearthed a small one on constructing your own racing dinghy. He realised that a modern ark would have to be substantially larger than this but we all have to start somewhere.

He spent the journey back to his home trying to list the number of breeding pairs of animals and birds he would have to accommodate. The fishes could presumably be left to their own devices. Insects, bugs and creepie-crawlies were too numerous to count. If only he had spent more time studying biology. Genes and stem cells thoroughly confused him, though they might be the answer to all the problems. Small amounts of genetic materials, properly stored … His head reeled and a wet and depressed man was eventually dropped by the local taxi firm on his doorstep and into Martha's arms.

She blamed herself. She shouldn't have let him go. He was getting too old and excitable for this sort of caper. She prescribed a whisky and soda, two aspirins and a good night's rest and returned to the crossword. Tomorrow she would extract an explanation.

Next morning, to a background of rain and sympathy, Martha gently probed her husband's condition. He could hardly contain his excitement but didn't wish to broach the subject just yet. Martha would probably think that it was another of his crazy fancies. At last her persistent questioning extracted the word.

"An ark, you say. It's a good idea, Bob, though you are not really the DIY type."

Her husband sighed. "I knew I could rely on you Martha to spot any difficulties."

"And there's another point, Bob. We would have to get a new cat. Poor old Pickles was neutered years ago."

Le Type Débrouillard
Birte Milne

Richard looked at the flashing message on his match.com account: 'A member has sent you a new message.' He couldn't believe how the messages just kept coming. All he had to do was pick and mix at his leisure. He clicked 'read message' and felt the familiar adrenaline rush as he skimmed through it. This one seemed absolutely perfect: Samantha – 35, blonde, 5'10", blue eyes, single (not divorced, separated or widowed). To top it all, she'd put 'high' by her income. He glanced through her personal statement and grinned quietly. He hadn't been wrong. She liked fine art, exotic holidays, drove a Ferrari. He could almost feel the wind against his face, sitting next to her in that red Ferrari. It just had to be red.

He clicked 'reply to message' and worked carefully on his answer. He had to touch just the right buttons to get a positive response to a suggested meeting after just one message. The QI Club always seemed to do the trick. His membership fee there had been worth every penny considering how much he'd got back in return; 'I'm a member of the QI Club' stood out in his personal statement and made him different from all the other sad weirdoes on the dating website. On top of that he actually really liked the place. It had an air of importance and glamour. He was one of 'them'. Being known and greeted by name when he came in for his usual drink after work gave him a real thrill and he'd made sure he knew the names of all the girls serving too, keeping the pretence going by tipping generously.

Samantha's reply came the next day. Richard rubbed his hands with excitement and anticipation. He had suppressed the urge to suggest a meeting the following day. Seeming too eager might put her off, but Saturday night – although only three days away – showed less desperation. He ate his usual beans on toast on a tray in front of EastEnders, but his mind kept travelling to his Saturday date and what was to come. He hadn't cut it this close before, but it had most certainly been a good move to wait for this one. She was just perfect.

He had to leave the bedsit by the end of the month, but hopefully he'd be all set up by then. The other final demands would have to wait and some he wouldn't have to pay at all when he moved in with her and left no forwarding address. He might even use a different surname. That had got him off the hook before and Samantha only had his first name. What sort of name would she like? It would have to be something really unusual, perhaps foreign. Perhaps his mother had lived in France and had an affair with a French Count and he was the result of their passion. She'd be sure to find that really romantic and impressive. Richard googled 'French Names' and scanned the list displayed. Would she like Pascal or perhaps Boucher? No, it had to be something more interesting and longer. Then he found it: Débrouillard. He said it out loudly a few times. Débrouillard. Richard Débrouillard. Just the ticket! It even had one of those fancy accents above the 'e'.

Saturday seemed to pass at a snail's pace. In the morning, Richard had gone for a jog and some fitness training in South Park which was the best he could do after he'd had to give up his gym membership. He'd had a long soak in the bath, going through his lines for the evening. He couldn't leave anything to chance and had prepared answers to any imaginable question he might be asked. He'd been quite amused by some of the outrageous questions his past dates had thought of and found the careful notes he'd compiled invaluable to avoid being cornered.

Clean, fresh and exfoliated, Richard carefully covered his body in self tanning lotion, watching out for the knees and elbows. Humming contentedly, while washing the lotion off his hands, he thought of the welcome he'd soon receive back at the tanning salon. Patience, patience he reminded himself. It may just take a few weeks to set this one up. While waiting for a deep tan to develop, Richard glanced at a few property magazines and checked his favourite internet shopping web sites. Soon he'd be able to open his account again, so he put a few items into the basket for later. At last it was time to get dressed. He'd already laid out his pressed and ironed dating gear.

"Not bad, my boy, not bad at all," he said, nodding to the mirror.

He arrived early at the QI. He wanted to have time to pick out just the right seats for their date. He liked to have the light behind him so his face was slightly shaded; he'd been told it gave him an air of mystery. It also gave him the advantage of being able to keep an eye on the entrance just in case someone should come he didn't want to be spotted by. He'd just taken a sip of the Bloody Mary China had brought him, when *she* walked in. Her picture hadn't done her full justice. The clinging silk of her dress showed off every slender curve of her size 8, 5 feet 10 inch figure, and the deep aqua was an exact match for her sparkling eyes. How could she have both the looks and the money? Normally he had to forget about looks and just focus on the money, but this time he had hit the jackpot.

With Samantha there would be no need to turn off the lights at bedtime or imagine other faces during love-making. This time the pleasure would be all his.

The evening went like a dream. He played her like a fiddle. Slowly, delicately, surely. She was bending, shaping, melting in his hands. He was good, no doubt about it, even if he had to say it himself. They'd had drinks, dinner and coffee in front of the open fire. He'd told her his story about his father, the French Count, and how he got the unusual surname. Then he told her how he was being made homeless because his building was being demolished. The story about wanting to give up his job because of sexual harassment by the boss had brought tears to Samantha's eyes. Now they were standing in Turl Street outside the club waiting for a taxi for Samantha. He never slept with his women on the first date, even though he found it hard not to make an exception this time. He'd just put her in the taxi, give her a goodnight kiss on the cheek and tell her he couldn't wait to see her again and that he'd phone her soon. Then he'd leave it a couple of days just to get her hot, before he went to phase two.

A car pulled up and stopped just in front of them. Not a taxi, but a police car. He hadn't noticed any trouble in the club. Samantha took his arm firmly, as two officers jumped out of the police car.

"Mr Richard Weston, I'm arresting you on suspicion of fraud and deception, of having used a false name to obtain money from several females, for aiding the suicide of a Miss Josephine Simons, and …"

Samantha's voice faded into a blur. Or was she really Samantha? And what about the red Ferrari?

*un type débrouillard – hustler (Collins Robert French Dictionary)

Turl Street Encounter
Yvonne Hands

It was fifty years since I had walked down Turl Street, Oxford. A lifetime ago. Nothing had changed. Three ancient colleges still filled the narrow road. Then, it was late May 1944 and I was in the uniform of the American Airborne, with Kate on my arm. Not quite so much on my arm as wrapped round me and I her, so that we could hardly walk. But we managed it. We could manage anything when the goal was her bedroom, just down the road. We only saw each other, nothing else mattered. Grey, war-time England in the fifth year of fighting for its life: the V-1s on London, my life in camp. I only saw Kate.

Suddenly my 1990's self was so overcome by the vividness of these memories, that I had to lean on the ancient wall before I could come back to the present. I was now here, in England, doing a course at the university in Oxford. I had never been back since leaving in '44. Indeed I had studiously avoided Europe, but this short course at one of the colleges had so appealed to me, that I decided that my 69-year-old self could face England again. I was now so shaken by my reaction that I wondered if it had been a good idea.

I had spent the first weeks of the course in the college, eating, studying and reading, very content. But today, one of my last days, I came looking. As I stood there, I saw the house on the corner where she had rented a room, the room of our love. Nostalgia and a kind of anguish swept over me in a way that I would not have thought possible after all these years. I pulled myself together and quite determinedly went to look at it. It was now a restaurant and I decided to eat there, to give in to – even wallow in – my memories, and have a last, nostalgic lunch.

There were a few people in the small, rather charming dining room: several couples, the odd lone tourist and one family party. The last thing I wanted was a lot of jolly bonhomie so I went to sit in a dark corner with my back to them. I needed to be alone with my thoughts. While I was eating I tried to work out the location of Kate's room. The room I was sitting in looked out onto the Master's lodgings of Jesus College and I remembered the great chestnut tree there, and how, in the war, the Master's wife had kept chickens in the garden. Looking out at the same chestnut, the cultivated chicken-less garden, I felt a longing sweep over me for that time.

Lying about my age, I had joined the forces at 17, wanting to be a pilot like my brother, but naturally I was put in the army. My brother was my hero. My father had died when I was nine and Jim, four years older than I, had taken on the role. I loved and admired everything about him, from the way he looked, the way he thought and the way he was. Jim had the family looks, very tall, fair, blue-eyed, rather square face, rather hook-nosed. And terribly handsome. From our family photographs I could see that same Brocklehurst face staring at me for over a hundred years. I actually took after my mother and was smaller and darker. When I was young I longed to look like Jim but, over the years, I had got used to my own appearance and even quite liked it. Anyway, Jim joined up immediately our war started and quite soon was in England and flying over Germany, writing long letters telling of his life. I hated being without him – he had filled the father role only too successfully – and longed to join him. I managed to get to England at the beginning of 1943 and for almost a year we saw a lot of each other, meeting frequently in London and having just the greatest and best of times. Then, at the end of 1943, he was killed, and I felt my life had ended too. He was my father, my adored brother, my best friend, my most admired and beloved person in the world. Fortunately, at that time my unit was very busy and work took over.

It was not long after he died that I met Kate. It really was love at first sight. I was walking down Turl Street, peering into a college, when I collided with someone. I had knocked into her quite hard and she almost fell. I grabbed hold of her and looked into an enchanting face. Green eyes looked rather sternly into mine and then smiled.

"Watch out, Yank! Don't knock the natives about."

From then on we were inseparable and all my free time was spent with her. She would talk about her life in Oxford generally and in Jesus College in particular, where she worked, about the dons she worked for. There was one particular one, Desmond, who was very keen on her. He was always asking her out and before she met me she had been out with him a bit. He always called her Kitty, though she told him how much she preferred Kate, but Desmond was the sort who was unchangeable. Poor old Desmond. He had been very anxious to join the services but his work as a scientist at the labs here was considered more important so that was where he had to stay. I was amused that my only rival was an Oxford don. I used to see him sometimes: a tall, round-faced, pink-cheeked Englishman – a good sort, I could see, but a bit of a loser I thought.

We lived a very quiet life. While the dance halls were filled with jitter-bugging Americans, our life in that room was all we wanted. We went out to eat sometimes, the poor war-time food, and Kate cooked a bit, but none of it seemed important, just our being together. Even as I sat there, fifty years later, I was swept by the joy, the ecstasy, the total peace and contentment that time held for me. What happened outside meant little to us: the V-1s raining on London, that this island was loaded with troops: Free French, Poles, Czechs, Americans, lining up for the invasion of Europe, that just over the water the whole of Europe, from France to the steppes was ruled over by the long, bloodied, grey wolf of the German Army, waiting to devour us.

I knew our days were numbered; we were preparing for the invasion and I would be in it. I told her I would be going shortly but that I would be back. I knew I was not going to die.

And that last time I walked down The Turl with her, I spent the night in her room and we talked on and off the whole night. How we would be married immediately I got back and how desolate poor Desmond would be when she left, how we would have children quite soon – she was longing to have children.

"I could be pregnant now," she said, giving me that slanting sideways look out of her green eyes. But I didn't take it seriously, knowing Kate.

"Great," I said. "I'll start collecting baby clothes." Kate always tended towards the dramatic. Though the most dramatic event of all, the coming invasion, she refused to talk about, she just closed up.

Well, I did go to Europe and I did not die, but I damn nearly did. The last thing I remember was the glider being cut away from the pilot plane, my heart thumping away, and the faces of the other men, as we glided down. Then all blacked out. I came to once; I was covered in blood, but totally clear in my mind. I was still sitting in the glider and so were all the others, quietly companionable, sitting together, some leaning cosily against their mates. Dressed to kill. All dead.

I knew nothing. Months went by before I was totally conscious. I had been very badly wounded, the only one to survive. I came out a different man, physically and mentally and I didn't recover my memory fully until two years later, but I had a wonderful nurse to whose care I owe my life. She knew I could not now have children, but loved me enough to say that having me was all she needed. We had a comfortable life. No, I never contacted Kate – what had I got to offer her? Yes, I felt I had let her down, done nothing for her. But that was later when I became more myself. And that feeling had grown with the years.

And I was sitting in her old room – I realised that the room I was eating in was just that – and looking out on precisely the same scene that we had done fifty years ago, from her bed, unchanged (apart from the chickens): the narrow street, the same two colleges, the great chestnut. And I was beginning to feel that same man again. But I knew this was a downward spiral and would lead nowhere; I pulled myself up and forced myself into the present. I became aware of the family party behind me which was getting quite boisterous with a lot of chaff and laughter. Apparently it was the birthday of one of them, and between all the hilarity I learned that there was an older couple and it was their son's 49th birthday, that his wife and children and a few friends were all celebrating this. He was a farmer apparently, living in a very rural area. Then, "Happy Birthday Jamie!" was sung and everyone joined in. Photographs were taken and the other diners were all asked to be part of the photograph. I half turned, not wanting to be drawn in, and had my photograph taken, then resumed my meal. I lingered a little, not wanting to say goodbye to the room, but eventually paid up and went out to the street.

I moved along the pavement carefully, side-stepping the rather drunken birthday party group who were just saying final farewells, when I felt a sharp knock and almost fell. I clutched desperately on to my assailant to stop myself falling over completely and I felt him really holding on to me, with the same idea. For a moment we clung together, then a rather charming voice said,

"I'm terribly sorry. I'm afraid I've drunk too much."

I looked up into his face and almost fell again. I looked straight into the Brocklehurst face, the face of so many old photographs of my family. Unmistakable. I was frozen there, unable to move, just peering into that face. Then I heard a woman's voice – a voice I knew – saying laughingly,

"Don't knock the natives over, Jamie." And, after a pause saying more sharply, as I still stood there, "Is he all right, Jamison? I think perhaps you've hurt him."

I knew exactly. In that flash I knew exactly what it all was. I was looking into the face of my son. In one second I felt complete joy, almost ecstasy, and I forced my eyes away and looked into the green eyes of the speaker, an attractive, charming, 68-year-old woman. The rather elderly, pink-cheeked man with her said,

"I think he's all right, Kitty."

I took one last look, taking in the three teenagers, all with Brocklehurst features. My grandchildren looked back at me with their blue eyes rather puzzled. Then, once more at my son, one last ecstatic, agonised look at my boy, then at Kate. I muttered something about it being my fault and moved on without a backward glance.

I went straight back to college, gathered up my things, took the first train out, took the first plane back to the U.S. and just sat in my apartment in Manhattan for a long time, still full of joy and despair. But fortified by the fact that I had at last done the right thing by Kate. I had left the family intact.

I thought of those – my – Brocklehurst children, living their safe and secure family life in their farm in the green English countryside. Yes, I thought, some corner of an English field will be forever foreign.

The Postman
M.S. Clary

The last time I walked down Elsinore Avenue, I saw that number 34 was up for sale. The garden looked neglected, dead leaves lay unswept in the porch. There didn't seem to be anybody about.

It's blowing from the west today. No matter how hard I try to spear these bits of rubbish, they whoosh off. Like they're having a laugh. Sweet wrappings, old envelopes. You wouldn't believe. Shan't have to bother with that one now, it's gone over the fence. Just hope the Boss Man wasn't watching.

The first time it happened, it was definitely an accident. I'd had a recurrence of that pain in my back. The sort of low down pain that never goes away, and always seems to catch you when you bend. My load had got unbearably heavy with all that junk mail they send out. Those catalogues that nobody asks for that just get thrown away. I'd been to see Dr Jones, and he'd put me on anti-depressants. I told him I was never depressed but he seemed to think they would relax my muscles and help with the pain. I'd already had a month off and was keen to get back to work, as, strange to tell, I was missing it. Anyway, put it down to the new tablets if you like, but on my way back to the Depot that morning I noticed there was a bunch of letters stuck at the bottom of the bag. I don't know how I'd missed them, but it was too late to do anything about it. Questions would have been asked. I parked up next to my car, and shoved them in the boot. I definitely intended to deliver them the following day.

"How's it going Jack?"

"Not too bad, Mr Howard."

"I'd like to get this area finished by lunch-time, if possible."

"No problem, Mr Howard."

I try to do my best for Mr Howard. His job is not an easy one.

A week later, I had a flat on the way home from work. I was searching in the boot for the jack, and there was the bundle of letters. I came over a bit shaky because in my fifteen years with the Post Office, I'd never failed to deliver a letter. I didn't know what to do. I drove around a bit, until the thought came to me that the best thing would be to take it all back to my flat, sort it out there, and just deliver what looked urgent. I found it quite easy. Anything that had been hand-written should go through on the grounds that it could be a birthday card for an elderly person, or perhaps a child. Or anything that looked official, like pensions or car tax that went without saying. But what I noticed was that nearly all the correspondence seemed to be in cellophane wrappers selling footwear or night attire. Or in white envelopes, advertising some nonsense from the banks, credit card companies and such. People were hardly going to miss that sort of thing were they? I took matters into my own hands and it didn't take long. But the problem was that it left a big pile of all the other stuff I wasn't sure what to do with. So I put them in a bin liner, and shoved it under the bed.

It should be time for a break soon. Mr Howard has been quite sympathetic about my back. Not like that bastard back at the Depot. I'll swear that when he knew it was playing up again, he put me on a new round on purpose. A big estate with lots of dead ends you couldn't turn the van in. I was having to carry everything on foot. It was then I really noticed the weight of the catalogues. Some houses had half a dozen delivered every day. What was the point? What benefit was this kind of mail to my customers? Despite the anti-depressants, I was starting to feel depressed. It all needed a re-think. One wet morning, I decided to pop home for a cup of tea. Put my feet up, watch 'Trisha'. She's good at solving people's problems. I did intend going out later and finishing the round, but I must have dozed off. When I came to, it was time to get back to the Depot to clock off. I looked at my bag and wondered what Trisha would have done. Anyway, I came up with my own solution and put it all with the first lot, under the bed.

After that, it became a bit of a habit. The strange thing was, nobody seemed to notice. I thought there would be lots of angry customers ringing in to find out where their letters had got to. But nothing happened. It was then that I realised that I had relieved a lot of people from a burden. They were not worried by the lack of post, but, like me, were experiencing a kind of a release.

My yellow plastic sack is nearly full now. I can see a few of the other chaps standing about having a cigarette. Sometimes I wonder what they did to end up here like me. Abducted a child perhaps, or robbed a bank. Though some do boast, it's one of the unwritten rules not to talk about it, 'specially not in front of Mr Howard. For my part, I came to look upon my misdemeanour as a form of social service. I was always scrupulous about anything that had to be signed for. And I never kept anything back for my own gain. That went in my favour. And I always kept a look out for anything that looked personal. But that came to be my undoing.

I had noticed there was a woman in Elsinore Avenue, number 34 (you'll have guessed), who often seemed to be waiting at her front door. She was nice and friendly, always smiled and said good morning. Even offered me a cup of tea once. I recall we had a nice chat about the weather. Some of the others would have thought it was a bit of a come-on, but she wasn't that type. She would be calling to the children to hurry up, or they'd be late for school. They were well-mannered kids too, not like those teenagers at the bus stop who used to shout out Postman Jack at me. But I didn't care for the husband. He never gave me a second glance as he drove off in his old grey Vauxhall. One day I realised I hadn't seen the car or the husband for quite a while. Something had happened. The children had started squabbling amongst themselves, and whenever I saw her, Mrs Smith just looked sad. She never offered me another cup of tea. I wondered whether she was waiting for a letter then one day I saw one addressed to her, hand-written, with a Derbyshire postmark. Curiosity got the better of me. Mr Smith had written to say that he wasn't coming back, said he had met somebody else, and would send some money when he could.

I couldn't let her read that, could I? I tore it up. It worried me. Then I got the idea of composing a few words to her myself. I told her that I had gone away to find work, and that I would send for her and the children soon. As an afterthought, I put in a ten-pound note. Then I drove to Oxford, and posted it in the Turl Street box.

Here comes Mr Howard again giving out more yellow sacks. I think he likes me. Well, I always do go that extra mile. I don't know whether there is a Mrs Howard at home. Sometimes he looks as if he'd enjoy a good chat, but he stays professional. Some of the lads here can hardly string a sentence together.

"How many more hours have you got with us, then Jack?"

"About two hundred and forty, Mr Howard."

"Better get going then Jack; slowing down won't make them go any faster."

"No, Mr Howard."

See what I mean?

I kept looking out for more letters from Mr Smith, but none came. This seemed very careless of him. I started to worry about her, and the kiddies. Sometimes I used to walk down Elsinore and have a peep in the window. I went over in the evenings too, just to see whether the Vauxhall had reappeared. I couldn't forget about that poor lady waiting for a letter telling her all about their new life together. I decided that it was time to write to her again.

Dear Evaline,

How I am missing you and your warm kisses. Tell the children I am longing to see them too. How is little Angel getting on at school? She must be getting good at her reading now. And what about my Big Boy? Does he still want to be a footballer when he grows up? Tell them I love them and we'll all be together again soon.

From your loving husband,

Tom xxx

(P.S. I am hoping to afford a new car soon.)

This time I enclosed a twenty-pound note. I suppose you could say I was becoming over-involved.

My back wasn't getting any better, and I began to enjoy my mornings at home. What with my daily visits to Elsinore I found myself getting exhausted. Stress they call it today. The pile of mail in my bedroom was getting so big, I had to start putting the overflow in the bathroom. One day, I took a pile to the tip. I tell you, it was a relief to see them go.

One weekend, I was walking past no 34, and saw Evaline in the garden. I waved and said hello, but she didn't reply. In fact, she seemed to turn away and hurry indoors. After what I'd been doing to help, I must say I felt a bit snubbed. I decided the time had come to try to explain things, to let her know that she had somebody on her side. I went and knocked on her front door. She opened it a crack and I asked her how she was and told her not to worry. I said I thought Mr Smith would be home soon. But she just shut the door. It was after my visit, I learned that she had called the Police.

They found over 100 sackfuls of undelivered post. Even to me, that came as a bit of a shock. Because of my previous good record, and poor health, I was sentenced to 400 hours of Service to the Community. That's how I come to be spending my days on the roadside, picking up litter. It's not too bad. It's been a revelation to me how much rubbish there is on our streets. I feel I am doing my bit for society.

I know I shall never see her again, but sometimes, on a fresh bright morning like this, I think of Evaline. She is smiling as she once used to smile at me, and the children are singing some jingle they've learned off the telly. The air is sweet as we join hands, and walk towards the park.

Would That It Were
Julie Adams

The three undergraduates were relieved to escape the hot June sunshine as they turned into the doorway of the QI Club, leaving the sweating tourists behind. They hurried upstairs past the 'Members Only' sign to the private rooms. The interior of the first floor was a well-preserved example of turn-of-the-millennium décor, with leather furniture, varnished floorboards, and noughties art on the muted walls. A variety of lamps complemented the light that came in at the tall Georgian windows from the narrow streets outside. The students headed for the quieter far corner and dropped onto squashy sofas. The two men reached up to undo white bow-ties and the top button of their wing-collared shirts.

"You girls get it so easy with *sub fusc*," complained Rupert, the taller, blond one. "You can basically wear anything as long as you remember to tie that ridiculous ribbon round your neck."

"Hello?" said the girl, waving her slim legs in the air like a distressed insect. "We all had to wear tights. In this weather."

"But aren't they all hi-tech, stay-cool, super-breathable fabrics nowadays, Caro?"

"My arse," said Caroline with feeling. "It's all just hype so they can charge 50 Euros a pair."

She slipped her hands under her black skirt, hooked her thumbs into the waistband of the tights and stripped them off, wriggling her bare thighs on the sofa's seat.

"Ooh, the leather's all cool," she sighed, her eyes nearly closed.

The young men gulped. A waitress approached, her black skirt and white shirt similar to the female undergraduate's formal garb. But without the cap and gown this townie didn't count. Nevertheless Rupert grabbed her hand and kissed the back of it.

"Sweet angel, bring me sustenance, for I have slaved in a hot examination hall this afternoon," he implored.

"What would you like?" asked the waitress, ignoring his behaviour. "Dinner doesn't start for another hour but the bar is open and we have a snack menu."

"Just bring us one of everything on the cocktails list, and three straws," said Henry with a straight face.

"Ignore them," said Caroline. "We'll start with a jug of Pimms while we decide on the rest."

The two young men followed Caroline's lead and threw their black gowns and jackets over the back of an adjacent armchair. Caroline looked at the hologram of Stephen Fry pointing at them and read aloud the speech bubble:

"Are You Quite Interesting?"

"I will be when I'm drunk," said Rupert and started to sing.

> "One more day to go,
> One more day of sorrow,
> One more day of dreadful Mods,
> and I'll be finished tomorrow."

The waitress returned with the Pimms and some locally grown olives.

"That will be 195 Euros, please."

"Put it on my member's account," said Rupert, pressing his right thumb into her payment terminal. There was a pause while they poured Pimms and took long gulps. Rupert broke the silence.

"Well, I didn't think that was too bad."

"Apart from the heat and the primitive toilet facilities," said Caro.

"It is all a bit twentieth century," agreed Henry.

"No, the exam paper I meant," continued Rupert. "I was fine on the impact of globalised governance but I couldn't remember when proportional representation was introduced."

"Duh!" chorused Henry and Caroline, inserting their tongues behind their respective lower lips. "When Lembit Opek was Prime Minister, of course."

"Oh yes, 'The Cheeky Premiership'," said Rupert, suddenly enlightened.

"With a grasp of the subject matter like that you could even aspire to a Desmond," sneered Caroline. She removed the red carnation from her commoner's gown and started to pull off the petals. "Anyone fancy tennis after Hall tonight?"

"No, I'll have my nose in my notes again," said Henry. "I can play as much tennis as I like all summer."

"And I've got the briefing for my space tourism trip. Reward from the Aged Ps for finishing the first year," Rupert said.

"What a complete waste of money, Roop," burst out Caroline. "You could just use the 3-D simulator in the JCR and go all the way to Pluto, not just a piffling trip beyond the stratosphere."

"It will look good on my CV when I apply for the Space Programme after we graduate."

Henry snorted. "Because a degree in PPE is the perfect preparation for being an astronaut."

Rupert launched into his usual defence of how professionals of all kinds were needed in the Space Corps nowadays but was cut short by the return of the waitress. She took their second order but reminded them they might be caught by University Proctors if seen drunk in public.

"Those mothers have tasers," said Henry with respect.

When the waitress brought their drinks she mentioned the forthcoming party.

"Will you be coming next weekend to celebrate our anniversary? It's fifty years since the QI was founded in 2003. We'll all be wearing noughties fancy dress."

"Super!"

"We'll be holding the party in Jimmy's," the waitress smiled. "We were starting to get short of room once the library upstairs was declared a national monument. But we can hold much larger events since we bought all the St James's buildings," she said, scoring a point in the unspoken Town versus Gown battle.

The three students avoided eye contact. It was still an immense embarrassment for the University that one of its oldest and best-known colleges had gone bankrupt. Some thought it a just reward for the academic and fiscal corruption of the college which admitted the fewest undergraduates from state schools. In a bid to change the subject Rupert asked,

"Will Sir Stephen be there?"

"Of course," replied the waitress. "He'll be bringing Lady Fry and all their children."

"It's such a romantic story," said Caroline wistfully. "Winning *Strictly Come Dancing* like that and marrying his dance partner."

"Imagine finding time to fit in all those rehearsals while you're Secretary General of the UN," said Rupert.

"How else do you fill your time once you've triumphantly reformed Britain's Education System *and* the NHS?" asked Henry rhetorically.

"And most of his friends are coming, too," the waitress continued. "Lord Chief Justice Clive Anderson, Jo Brand – the Poet Laureate – Dame Sandi Toksvig, Lord Alan Davies of Loughton ..."

"Our longest-serving Prime Minister," interrupted Henry. "Our tutor goes seriously postal every time someone mentions the General Ignorance Party."

Caroline shuddered. "I can't watch those early editions of the quiz without thinking of what we know about Bill Bailey now."

"Who'd have thought it?" agreed Rupert, shaking his head. "But I still love that episode they broadcast from the surface of the Moon." He looked at his personal chronometer.

"Time to beetle off for Hall, Chaps and Chapesses."

The waitress smiled as she retrieved a notebook from behind the bar. She just had time to scribble a few field notes before the evening rush started. She grinned more widely at the thought of the twittish one competing against the world's brightest engineers and scientists to apply for the Space Corps. Other club members had told her that, on being given a car for his 18th birthday, Rupert had asked,

"Does it come with a chauffeur, or do I have to learn to drive?"

His admission to the University had been eased by the skill of the Oxbridge Entrance Tutor (paid by results) at his sixth form crammer, with further lubrication provided by the foresightful donations of several generations of his ancestors.

As for the smaller youth, there wouldn't be much time for tennis between shifts at the warehouse distribution centre near Doncaster where he had a summer job supplementing his scholarship. She was fairly sure that he still kept secret his origins from a depressed former mining village. That one, the waitress thought, was potentially the leader of Britain's next revolution.

The girl was equally interesting. During Michaelmas term she had been seen snogging with so many different men in the dark corners of the Vodka Bar downstairs that the Club's staff thought she must be on the game. Known as a 'horizontal scholarship', it wasn't an uncommon method of funding higher education. But it had transpired that she was just acting out her teenage rebellion before going back to Mummy's bishopric during the hols.

The waitress tucked her notebook out of sight again. Her PhD on 'The Social Construction of Middle-Class Ethnicities' was shaping up nicely. The next time they had a tutorial at Brookes she was sure that Professor Fry would find the latest data, well, quite interesting.

Friends Revisited
Margaret Wilcox

Grace paused, about to cross Turl Street; the door just across the road was beckoning. It was good to be home. As the hurrying students flowed round her in their urgent quest for lunch, Grace crossed the road and walked through the door. She was cheerily greeted by a waiter which confused her. Grace had never seen him before but he seemed to know her. He ushered her to a table in a bar and put a Babycham in front of her. Grace never knew there was a bar in the building. How had they missed it?

"Is this new?" she inquired of the waiter.

He just smiled and nodded. Several students sat round a table laughing uproariously at some joke or other. How she wished she could join in and laugh with them. Betty, Joan and Peggy sat down at the table with her and the waiter put Babychams in front of them all.

"Isn't this fun?" she greeted them.

They agreed and tried to work out where the Indian Restaurant had gone. Their rooms were at the top of the building but they didn't mind the stairs. They reckoned the exercise was good for them; they had to do something to work off the curries they were fed by Anna, the matriarch of the family. Pleased to have feminine company Anna had taken them under her wing and saw they never went hungry.

They watched the male students coming in and commented on how handsome they considered them and criticised the clothes of the girls. Some more students came in and Peggy said to Grace,

"Hasn't he got a big nose?"

Grace, shocked, retorted, "He can't help it!"

Realising she had spoken rather sharply, Grace added,

"The same as I can't help being so beautiful, with a wonderful figure and …"

They all laughed or groaned and Betty flicked Babycham at Grace. Betty and Peggy were talking about their hair. They both had bouffant hair styles, obtained by vigorous back-combing and lots of hair lacquer. Peggy's mousy hair was given help with a bottle of peroxide, but because of this her hair had became brittle and the back-combing broke the hairs. She never needed to have it cut; it just broke off. Joan's hair was a marvellous beehive. With her hair piled on top of her head, held in place by grips, combs and lacquer she said she never had to do her hair in the mornings. She just had to be careful how she slept. Grace felt she couldn't live with hair like any of her friends. She hated fuss and hairdressers. Her hair was red. There are many names for the colour but she just called it red. It was thick, envied by Peggy, and curly. She used an Alice band to keep it off her face and when it got too long, Grace just cut it herself. Hairdressers were so expensive and every customer tended to come out looking the same.

Peggy suddenly clutched Grace's hand staring at the door. Grace looked and *he* was framed in the doorway. This was Peggy's latest love of her life. She was besotted. Grace was concerned about this and hoped Peggy didn't make the same mistake as Gwen. She had gone off somewhere to have the baby which was adopted. So sad! Helen had been lucky though. Her boyfriend was the responsible sort and they married in haste. Grace hoped they wouldn't repent at leisure. Peggy's beau had dark good looks and such deep brown eyes. His smile, which he used all the time, melted the stoniest heart. They both left the table to go to their next lecture and Betty suddenly looked at her watch and gasped.

"I've missed my tutorial. What shall I do?"

"Just say the queue for lunch was long," Joan advised her.

Joan never arrived anywhere on time but never seemed to get into trouble like the rest. It's not fair, but life wasn't fair, was it?

Someone else was coming through the door and Grace caught her breath. He was tall, blond and very, very handsome. Standing there he turned many heads as he checked round the tables until he saw Grace. The smile he gave her made her heart stop. The blue eyes twinkled and the nicely proportioned mouth tweaked at the corners. He walked to the bar, asked the barman how much the tab was and settled up. He came over to Grace and sat in Joan's chair. He put his large hand over hers.

"Have a good morning, Granny?" he asked.

Where had Joan and Betty gone? They must have seen him come in. That's real friendship to leave when her special man came in. No, Grace felt that wasn't quite right. She wasn't sure what was right though. She felt fuzzy.

"Must have had too much to drink," she muttered. "Only three though."

"Come on," he said getting to his feet.

"If you don't mind me asking …?" the barman started politely as they walked past him on the way to the door. "What would you do if the old lady didn't come here?"

Grace's handsome escort replied, "Panic I expect, but she always will. The times she can remember are here, where she was happy. She used to live here with her friends before it was the QI Club."

He led Grace out of the door into the sunshine.

"The car's by Blackwell's," he said. "Mum's been very worried."

Things were beginning to happen to Grace's thoughts. What had happened? Mum? Grace never knew her husband's Mum. Where did Joan and Betty go? Then Grace grasped a thought from the muddle.

"You're so like your father."

He smiled down at Grace. "Grandfather," he said gently. "I knew I'd find you at the QI Club."

"I was happy there," Grace told him. "It's nice to see my friends again."

Through the Pane
Birte Milne

Through the soapy window I can just make out the shape of her moving figure. She is wearing black as always, but the long flowing skirt is a change from the usual, showing off her slender ankles and a pierced belly button under a cropped top. My eyes are drawn towards the hypnotic sparkling white stone dancing amongst the parting curtains of foam, as the soap glides slowly down the window pane, impatiently waiting for my scraper to remove every bubble before hitting the pavement below.

I have to tear myself away from the white stone, back to the remaining soap and the scraper poised in the top left corner of the window. Most of the soap has hit the pavement and a few suds have already dried hard. I'll have to soap the window again to get the proper sparkle. Anybody inside the bookshop is bound to notice the repeat soaping and make some comment or joke when I get inside. At least I have a few minutes to work out an excuse and make up some clever comment. I finish the window, the last on the outside, humming softly in unison with my iPod.

> 'And I'd give up forever to touch you
> Cause I know that you feel me somehow
> You're the closest to heaven that I'll ever be
> And I don't want to go home right now'

Oh, if only you knew, Iris. If only you didn't look straight through me as well as the window pane.

I keep on humming as I check the finished window. Her smiling face is doing a miming act on the other side of the glass pane. I give her a blushing, flustered smile back, before picking up the bucket, ready to make my way inside. This is the first time she has seen me. Actually looked at me. Chills run down my spine and the humming fails to make it past my throat. Nobody has had that effect on me since I was 17, but she has brought all the forgotten feelings of teenage angst out in my 31-year-old body. I take a deep breath and walk quasi-cheerfully with my bucket through the front doors of the QI Club, turning left into the bookshop.

"OK if I do you on the inside now?" As soon as the words leave my mouth, I want to take them back.

"Well, there's an offer I can't refuse." She looks at me quizzically, waiting for my response.

I struggle to move my gaze from her lips; they seem to be fighting a losing battle, trying to remain serious. She's flirting with me.

"Erm … I… You know… ehh… what I mean."

I hurry to the window furthest from her mesmerising eyes, still feeling them warming my back, but at least my burning cheeks are hidden from her view.

A customer comes into the shop. Her eyes turn away from my shoulders and I instantly feel the loss of their touch. A multitude of unanswered and unanswerable questions sweep though my mind as I begin the precarious task of soaping the window while carefully avoiding book displays and Venetian blinds.

Was she really flirting? She surely can't fancy me? … Can she? She is bound to have a boyfriend? I wouldn't be her type anyway? Oh, God. I can't think. … Help!!!!

I am at the third window now. More than halfway. I have to say something soon, before it's too late. But what? Ask her where she's from. What her name is. Anything safe. Test the water first and see how she responds. I'm on the last window. Time is running out. I take a deep breath and count to ten.

"How long have you been working at the QI … book … shop?"

My words hang in the air as I look round the shop for her familiar figure.

She's gone. In her place is a bespectacled, nerdy-looking chap. He looks at me with surprise but answers me politely, obviously pleased that someone has paid him attention.

"I've only been here for two weeks. Still getting used to all the titles and names of authors and the till. Been good, so far, though."

His voice drones on behind me while I finish the last window. I give him an occasional nod and shrugging of shoulders to acknowledge that I'm listening, but my thoughts are far, far away. Where did she go? She didn't say goodbye. Is she coming back? The 'nerd's' voice reaches me again just as I pick up the bucket and make ready to leave.

"Tanya's been really great, helping me with everything. Shame she's going back to Ukraine or Slovakia or wherever it is she's from. I'll miss her…"

Tanya? Her name is Tanya. I feel the hardness of my teeth against my tongue as I whisper her name. For the past few months I have watched her undisturbed from outside the window. I know a little about her yet there is so much more I want to find out. Through the pane, I've seen her sad eyes looking longingly at books of faraway lakes and mountains, caressing the pages lovingly before sliding them secretly into her bag. Other times I see her returning them rapidly to the shelves with anxious glances towards the door. When she's alone, her face and features are marked by foreign hardship and I sense the pain of unhealed wounds deep within her.

I call her Iris, after the song, mainly, but also for the colour of her eyes. Those mesmerising, longing openings to her soul. The colour changes to sparkling, deep lapis lazuli at other vivid, vibrant moments, when she's not alone. I have wanted to be there with her for so long, to smooth the lines on her forehead and ease the pain from her shoulders; to make the vibrant sparkling moments of lapis lazuli break through the sadness and become lost in the depth of the bottomless blue.

I give a parting nod to the 'nerd', as I leave the bookshop with my bucket. This is me done. Finished. I walk slowly out of the QI Club, hoping to get one more, last glance of her before I go. As the glass door swings shut behind me, I pause for a moment on the step, reluctant to leave her without any answers.

But the moment has passed. It never was. She's gone. Tanya. To me, you will always be – Iris.

Words taken from the song: 'Iris'; Music and lyrics by Johnny Rzeznik

Beauty is in the Eye
Jeni Bee

Elliot Fraser hadn't intended eating any lunch at all. The trouble was, he was in the QI bookshop when the smell of something delicious floated in from the café. It smelled like pasta and pizza, peppers and basil, and some unidentifiable tempting aromas all rolled into one. Go on, he told himself. You're sick of beans on toast. Go wild, mate.

He had been researching 'Abstract Expressionism in Literary Movements' which was his latest project's subtitle. The research postgraduate contract didn't pay a lot so Elliot had to watch his pennies but quite honestly he wasn't particularly enjoying this latest probe into the literary world. Studying the work of the New York School of Writers was tedious. He'd needed to give himself a good talking-to before he had even got out of bed. Now he felt like a break and food would be welcome. Yes, it would be a reward for the morning's efforts. He stared at his watch. Unbelievable! He'd only been working for thirty-five minutes.

Elliot bundled up his papers and made his way along to the café. He sat down on one of the brown leather bench seats and gazed up at the cheerful face of Stephen Fry blown up in a frame facing him. He wondered if the famous founder ever visited the QI. He doubted it. London was more than likely where he hung out.

The café was very quiet, unusually so at that moment, just the noise of crockery and saucepans in the back. Of course he was early. There was life there somewhere and the smells were stronger now he was nearer to them.

He suddenly realised he wasn't the only person sitting at a table. There was a girl with her back to him. She had the longest chestnut hair he had ever seen. He wanted to run his fingers through its silkiness. A student, he presumed.

His love life was non-existent. Samantha had dumped him for no good reason other than she thought their relationship was going nowhere. So what? What did she expect from a penniless graduate who was earning peanuts? She said he spent too much time on his appearance. Did she want a tatty unwashed dork? Anyway, she was past history now like all the others.

He fiddled with the table mat in front of him and wondered if he should call out for some service or try to chat up the unknown girl with the beautiful hair? Or should he go to The Kings Arms for a beer instead? Life had so many possibilities. It was easy to choose the wrong option and he'd certainly made some horrible choices recently. Things could only get better.

He considered his next line of work. Dystopia in novels. That was the title he'd been given for his research. It appealed to him. Dystopia, the supposedly evil twin of Utopia. He planned to study Tolkien, Orwell and Huxley, each one's writing noted for its sinister elements. He found the prospect of examining wickedness in literature fascinating, even though it would be purely fictional. He felt that recently he'd been living in Dystopia because everything around him was as bad as it could be. He was certainly due for a utopian experience. This could be the start of it.

He looked up as a waitress hovered over him. He knew her. She was a student at St Hilda's and worked in the café out of term time.

"Hi Jo!"

"Elliot! Haven't seen you in here for a while."

"No money. Splashing out today." He scanned the wall for the day's specials. "I'll have the cod and mash and a beer. Starving!"

She smiled. "None of our meals are very large. Quality not quantity here."

Elliot laughed. "Next time McDonald's then."

He was served quickly. Jo was right. The cod was small, piled on an equally small mound of potato and spinach. Delicious admittedly, but he'd eaten it in about four mouthfuls. The chestnut-haired girl appeared to have eaten and drunk whatever she'd got in front of her. Elliot hoped she might have turned round but no luck. He tapped her shoulder.

"Quiet in here, isn't it?"

For a moment there was no response. Then her head turned slightly.

"I like quiet," she said. Her voice was silky like her hair. She suddenly swung round on her chair to face him.

Her face was bony, the skin papery and wrinkled like a battered parcel. Her eyes bulged darkly. Elliot couldn't see what colour they were. She had no eyebrows, no eyelashes. Her lips were thin like a stretched rubber band. He stood up. Felt an urge to get away.

"Why don't you come and join me?" she asked. She had hardly any teeth, only a few spread-out black stumps.

He wanted to shout out that she scared the shit out of him, but all he could do was mumble, "I'm sorry I have to leave." He made his way to the kitchen door. "Can I pay now, Jo?" He almost felt desperate. Jo appeared with his bill and he handed her his credit card and she disappeared in the back. When he turned round the girl had left. He instantly regretted not joining her. She might have been an interesting person.

Jo returned with the card. Elliot immediately thought about trying to date her.

"Quiet in here," he said, "with just me and that girl. You might as well go home. Or come out with me."

"What girl?" She ignored the invitation.

"That girl with the long brown hair, sitting with her back to me."

"Elliot, you were the only person here."

"But ... she was definitely there. She spoke to me. You must have served her."

Jo laughed. "Too much vino last night?"

Elliot didn't reply.

"QI ghost?" She was grinning as she spoke.

"Is there one?"

"Supposed to be. Never seen it myself." Jo waved his credit card in front of him. "Anyway the machine's just rejected your card. Got any cash?"

Elliot was positive he'd got at least fifty pounds in his account. He furiously rooted around for some money and was left with a 5p piece. Gloomily he made his way up to the gents. Coming out was Rupert who was working temporarily in the library.

"Hi Rupert, got any info on the QI?" Elliot needed to check out the girl mystery.

"Not much. Only one book as far as I know. Is this part of the study you were doing this morning?"

"No. Just interested."

"I'll sort the book out for you if you're coming back in."

"Yes, I am. Thanks. You didn't see a young girl with long brown hair go past the library, did you?"

"No. Nobody's been in this morning, apart from you ... as far as I know. But I've been out a couple of times."

Two minutes later Elliot hurried down the stairs and it must have been almost at the bottom when he missed his footing and twisted his ankle. He hobbled into the bookshop, swearing. Not my lucky day, he thought. He flopped down into a chair and Rupert brought him the book entitled '*History of the QI building*'.

Trying to take his mind off the pain, Elliot glossed over the table of contents until he saw what he'd been looking for. '*Mary Makepeace, QI ghost*,' he read. A haunting! That's what he'd suspected. Ghosts didn't have to appear in the dark, did they? There were no rules as far as he knew. He felt a surge of excitement. It appeared that young Mary had been disfigured in a fire incident in 1790. No one wanted to marry her. Not only was she ugly, she was said to be 'barren as the desert.' The only part of her that grew normally again was her hair. She eventually threw herself off Magdalen Bridge and her body was found floating in the River Cherwell. Her ghost was said to appear to handsome young men who visited the QI Club where she'd once lived. If they refused her advances, then bad luck would befall them. One such fellow was said to have 'died by the sword' shortly after being approached by her in the year of her drowning.

Elliot shut the book and mulled over what he'd read. He had to admit he was probably considered handsome and the girl had approached him and he'd rejected her. But he certainly didn't believe in ghosts. No way! That girl was real. She felt real. He'd touched her. And as for that bad luck rubbish … Coincidence more like! He stood up and handed the book back.

"Interesting?" Rupert replaced the book in the history section.

"Yes … thanks. See you."

Elliot, still in pain, stepped into Turl Street, and recovered his bike he'd left chained outside. There was no way he could ride it when his ankle hurt so much. It was as he pushed it along the pavement that a car door suddenly opened and knocked him over, bike and all. Rupert, who'd heard a commotion outside, came to see what was up. He looked at Elliot who was lying there his face covered in blood.

"Bad luck," he said to the stunned body who was trying to speak. "Your front tooth's all chipped."

*

Elliot came out of the dentist's feeling elated because at last he was restored to his natural good looks. After his accident, he'd avoided looking at his face in the mirror, which wasn't easy because he always said something complimentary to his reflection. Like "cool," "fantastic!" or "Hey man, looking good." His reflection would now smile back at him and he didn't have to clean his teeth with the light off any more.

He felt like running down Turl Street and shouting, "Woweeee!" He was back in Utopia. He'd had all that treatment which hadn't cost him a penny. The woman who'd knocked him off his bike had to fork out. Well actually her insurance company did, which was just as well because Elliot only had a 5p piece to his name.

He thought back to that awful day of the accident. The rejected credit card, spraining his ankle, and then all this business with the chipped tooth. Anyway that was in the past, a dystopic day if ever there was one. He looked in the window of the expensive jewellers, catching a shaft of sunlight which lit up his face. He bared his teeth rather like the lion he'd seen at the beginning of old black and white movies. Brilliant! He couldn't see the join in his capped tooth. He ran his tongue over the repair. Smooth! The jagged bit had really freaked him out. A shadow passed behind him masking the excellent view.

"Hello Elliot," it said.

He swung round. It was the long-haired girl in the QI café. He realised he'd only seen her sitting down before. She was tiny and slender, almost childlike. He wondered how he could avoid staring at her face, especially when they were obviously going to have a conversation. A thought puzzled him.

"How do you know my name?"

"In the café. The waitress called you by name."

"Oh, yes. Of course ... what's yours?"

The thin lips smiled. "Maria Harmony," she told him.

"That's a beautiful name. I've never heard a name so beautiful." He looked at the Turl Street cobbles and tried not to focus on the bulging eyes.

"Thank you, Elliot."

They began walking together, chatting amiably. It seemed the natural thing to do.

"Are you a student?" he asked.

"No. I'm a searcher," she told him.

"How odd, that's what I do. I'm researching literature topics."

"No, Elliot. I'm not a *re*-searcher. I search for people. I'm striving to find someone at the moment."

"Oh ... a sort of private detective agency?"

"I suppose that's how you could describe it."

"Sounds interesting. Are you going anywhere in particular just now, Maria?"

"No."

"Shall we go for a drink somewhere? I'd like to get to know you better."

"Thank you, but I'd rather just talk if you don't mind. But not about me."

Elliot was relieved she'd said that when he remembered his lack of money. Couldn't expect her to pay. Come to think of it, she wasn't carrying anything like a purse or handbag. No visible pockets either. She was wearing an ankle-length flowery dress and an ancient-looking grey cardigan which draped over her bony shoulders like a shroud. Oh no! There he was again, back on the ghost idea. This girl was real. How could he have thought otherwise?

"I thought you were a ghost when I met you in the café."

There, he'd said it now. Probably unwise. Not very complimentary. But it was out now.

"Why?" She looked up at him. She reminded him of a hobbit, so small and somehow grotesque.

"Because Jo the waitress said I was the only one there. She was adamant."

"Don't worry Elliot, I seem to be invisible to most people. It's my face you see. They're embarrassed. Pretend I'm not there. In their mind, I don't exist."

The narrow mouth sagged. Elliot didn't know what to say. It was true but somehow she was fascinating, so gentle, so vulnerable.

"Did you have an accident or something? … Oh, look, I'm sorry. I shouldn't have asked that. None of my business. You don't have to answer."

She smiled. "Don't worry Elliot. It's not a secret. Yes, it was an accident. A fire actually. But please don't let's dwell on my problems. I want to be happy today."

His mind was racing. A fire! Too much of a similarity with the Mary Makepeace story. Or was it just a coincidence? He had to know.

As they walked down Cornmarket, he noticed an empty bench. He took her hand.

"Come on. Let's sit down." They sat, her tiny feet hardly touching the ground.

"I'm glad we met again, Maria. I'm sure I must have appeared very rude in the café. Now I can get to know you better. Do you live and work round here?"

He knew instantly he'd made a mistake questioning her again, when he saw the sorrow in her eyes. She'd insisted she didn't want to talk about herself and now he'd blown it. She stared up at him, a tear dribbling its way down the creases in her cheek.

"Sorry Maria. I'm a thoughtless prat." He put his arm around the thin shoulders, over the chestnut hair, and the tear disappeared.

An elderly woman carrying a load of Primark bags, puffed her way past the bench. She suddenly turned round, looked at the bench, walked across and sat down next to him. With a jolt he realised she was now sitting in Maria's place and Maria had melted away into nothing. He tried to keep the image of what had happened in his mind. It had reminded him of one of those lava lamps he'd seen at his grandmother's house. As a child, he'd been fascinated by the gooey green swirling mass inside. Maria's vanishing had been similar, not green, but a surge of white light, spinning into invisibility.

"Maria!" He called out her name. Could she still hear him? Was her spirit still there beside him? He felt nothing.

The woman regarded him suspiciously. "No, I'm Beryl actually," she told him.

*

Elliot couldn't sleep. He'd had the pillow in what seemed like a hundred different positions. Finally he tossed it across the room and got up to make himself a cup of cocoa. The milk smelt a bit off but he was past caring.

He wondered if he was going slowly mad. No, because as someone once said, anyone who really is going mad doesn't realise it. Hallucinating? He'd given up drugs after his first year in college. Overwork? Laughable! No, whichever way you looked at it, he had made friends with a ghost.

There was something compelling about Maria Harmony. Of course that wasn't her real name was it? He'd worked that one out around 3am. Mary had become Maria and Makepeace had become Harmony. Clever stuff. And she didn't want to know anything about him. Hadn't asked a single question. Did that mean she knew everything already? Scary! She might be able to see him doing all kinds of unmentionable male things. Maybe she could see him right now.

He called her name softly. There was no response. All he could hear were some birds serenading him from the chestnut tree outside his bedroom window. He opened the window and called her again ... nothing.

Things would be different now. He had seen her disappear. She couldn't go on pretending any longer. He kicked the edge of the bed. Why hadn't she told him the truth? Why hadn't she admitted she was a ghost? Didn't she know he'd been reading up about the QI ghost? There were so many unanswered questions. She was getting to him. He drifted off into a troubled sleep.

He was awakened by his mobile phone jangling on the table next to his bed.

"Hello."

"Hello darling. Hope I'm not too early."

"Mum!" He looked at his watch. Midday. "No. I was going to phone you anyway. I know it's always the same old story but could you lend me twenty pounds till the end of the month?"

"Of course, darling. Why don't you come home for the weekend? That's what I was phoning you about. Your grandfather is coming to stay and I know he'd love to see you."

Elliot's grandfather had always been there for him and Elliot was fond of him. Besides he needed to get away for some breathing space.

"I might well do that, Mum."

"Good ... Now Elliot is there anyone you'd like to bring with you?"

"No."

Typical Mum. Always hopeful. She didn't seem to realise he was only twenty-four. Taking someone home was a bit of a serious thing for the girl, well that was his experience anyway. The last one had been looking at glossy bridal magazines in W.H. Smith after he'd taken her to 'meet the parents'. Too close for comfort. He had no intention of settling down.

"Oh all right, darling. Promise you'll come?"

"I promise."

He splashed his face with water and dressed aimlessly, found a yoghurt past its sell-by date and grabbed an apple. Five minutes later, he made his way to Turl Street. That's where he'd seen Maria twice before. Maybe he would be lucky again. He wanted to see her more than anything.

The street was crowded with Saturday shoppers. He paused to look in the window of Past Times, selling its reproduction goods of bygone eras. A suitable place to find Maria, he wondered. She would have been living in Jane Austen's times, he supposed. He'd studied all the books and seen all the films. A wonderful era he could identify with. There was no sign of Maria.

He'd intended catching the train home before this. He knew they wouldn't have a meal without him and he suddenly remembered he'd got no money for the rail fare. His student railcard had expired and he hadn't bothered to renew it. He'd have to borrow the money, but where from? He could ask Rupert, the QI temporary librarian. He might still be there. Worth trying anyway. He pushed open the door and almost knocked over the girl coming out.

"Maria!"

"Hello Elliot. I think I owe you an apology. You need an explanation." Her wizened face crumpled.

"Never mind that now ... Come home with me ... to my parents." He couldn't believe he'd just said that.

"What?" They stood at the bottom of the stairs facing each other.

"Come on Maria. You owe me. Stringing me along with that denial!"

"All right, but they won't be able to see me. You know that, don't you?"

"Yes, of course, I've twigged that one by now. That doesn't matter. I will be able to see you ... Look we have to go by train. The only problem is I've got no money and I don't suppose you ghosts have any about your persons."

"What about your credit card?"

"No go. It's been rejected."

"I think you'll find it works again." She started laughing.

"What? Why you little ... It was you all the time causing me trouble."

"Yes. I didn't like you very much then."

"I suppose I was rotten to you."

"Yes."

"Come on!" Elliot decided not to dwell on that one. "Let's go."

They headed for the train station, hand in hand.

*

Oxford train station was crowded. Elliot had to queue for his ticket but nothing seemed to matter with Maria beside him.

"Aren't I the lucky one?" He looked down at the tiny figure. "You're the cheapest girlfriend I've ever had. Nothing to pay for, only one of everything."

"Girlfriend? Am I your girlfriend then?"

"Course you are." He squeezed her hand, thinking how easy it would be to accidentally crush the delicate fingers.

"Am I your girl because I don't cost you anything?" The creases in her brow were all screwed up, making her face even more ancient-looking beneath the silken hair.

Elliot laughed. "You're a funny old thing. No, it's because I like being with you. I'm pleased you found me again and gave me a second chance."

"But I am so ugly, Elliot. You could have a pretty girl."

"I don't want anyone but you, Maria. Honestly." It was true. He'd almost accepted her grotesque appearance. Didn't think it important to him.

They found an empty compartment and Elliot gave Maria his rucksack to keep on her lap so nobody would sit there. He didn't want to lose her again.

"If the train gets full you can sit on my lap," he told her.

"I'd like that," she said.

"Can I ask you questions please, Maria? I mean, is it all right to quiz you now I know you really are a ghost?"

Maria frowned again. "I'm not a ghost. I've been meaning to tell you that. I'm officially a Lost Soul. Ghosts just appear and disappear. I'm able to take on the human form of a girl of the present day, whatever time that might be. I can do many things ghosts can't do."

"Like?"

"I can influence lives a little."

"You mean like the credit card business, hurting my ankle and the accident with the bike."

"Credit card, yes. The others I didn't know about. I don't hurt people physically."

"I'll have to watch my step anyway, won't I?" He winked at her.

"Oh no! You've more than made up for your first rejection of me." She paused. "Elliot, I know you've read that story about me, but you mustn't believe everything you read."

"You mean it's not true?"

"Parts of it are. I was born Mary Makepeace, but here in the twenty-first century I've become Maria Harmony. Not many young people are called Mary Makepeace these days are they?

"No, I suppose not."

Elliot wondered if the suicide bit was true, but now didn't seem the right moment to ask. Or any moment if it came to that.

"I expect you're wondering about the suicide allegation?" It was as if she knew what was in his mind.

"Yes, but you don't have to tell me if you don't want to."

"I must tell you because that part is not true. I was walking by the river, missed my footing, and fell to my death. Everyone assumed it was suicide because of the effects of the fire and my disfigurement and misery. No man would look at me and I resented that. I wanted people to see beyond the ugliness. I was certainly depressed but I would never have taken my own life. That would have been cowardly."

Just at that moment a man got into the train and sat opposite Elliot and the rucksack. He took out a newspaper. Elliot realised he couldn't talk to Maria any more. The man could not have intervened at a worse moment, just as she was beginning to open up to him. Then almost at once he had an idea. He got out his mobile and pressed a few random buttons.

"That you, Maria?

"Yes, Elliot." She was giggling now.

"I'm speaking to you from the train on the way to my parents. I'm glad you're coming to meet them and my grandfather, too."

"Yes. I am happy, even though I cannot communicate with them. I am looking forward to observing them."

"You won't disappear on me this time, will you?"

"Not if I can avoid it. Sometimes I can't help it. It depends on the circumstances."

"Like the time that woman sat on you."

"That's right. It was out of my control."

The man opposite, who was only hearing one side of the conversation, was staring across at Elliot over his newspaper. Elliot was enjoying being centre stage.

"You'll have to stay in my bedroom tonight. Is that agreed?"

"Well, I think that is the usual procedure for girlfriends in these times, isn't it?"

"Definitely! And my parents won't know a thing about it."

"Do you think it is right to deceive them like this?"

"Absolutely! They wouldn't understand the fact I was sleeping with a Lost Soul. Are you happy with that arrangement, Maria?"

"Absolutely, Elliot."

Elliot suddenly burst into uncontrollable laughter. The man coughed loudly, making his newspaper rustle violently.

Elliot found his voice again. "I'll be getting out at the next stop, Maria. Bye! See you soon."

He clicked off and got up as the train pulled into the station. The rucksack rose into the air and followed Elliot to the carriage door. Elliot grabbed it and slung it over his shoulder. Behind him, the man blinked a few times, got up and tapped Elliot on the shoulder.

"Excuse me, but how did you do that brilliant trick with the rucksack?"

"I'm afraid that's my little secret," said Elliot.

*

Margaret Fraser uncrossed her legs determinedly and leaned forward in the armchair. She was worried about her son. Elliot had always been a bit of an enigma and since he arrived home earlier that evening she had seen even more evidence of this.

Her husband and father were preoccupied, Greg reading *The Times* and Norman was snoring quietly after the meal. Elliot had gone out for a walk even though it was raining.

"It's weird," she announced to the silent assembled company. No reply ... Typical men, she thought.

Greg raised an eyebrow over the top of his newspaper. "Yes? What is?"

"Elliot." She pushed her fingers through her bob of blonde hair.

"Elliot?" He wondered what she was on about. Female intuition again, he supposed. He sometimes wished that they'd had another child. Maggie was obsessed with their son, doted on his every word and gushed around any girlfriend who visited. Embarrassing. She couldn't see it of course. He couldn't understand how she could spend so much time on thinking about Elliot when she had such a demanding job. Head of department in the local comp for two years now.

"Yes. He's been acting very oddly since he arrived."

"Seemed fine to me." Greg tried to return to his reading.

"Well, he would. You don't notice things."

Norman opened one eye. "Leave the boy alone. You two don't know you're born. A son who got a First at Oxford and still visits you! He's a good lad, is Elliot. What more do you want?"

"Dad, I know all that, but there's something stranger about him this visit."

"Such as?" Greg knew he and his father-in-law would have to listen. Maggie had made up her mind.

"Well, when he arrived I saw him coming down the path and he had his arm stretched out. He kept it there all the way down until I opened the door."

"Oh Maggie, this is ridiculous. Perhaps his arm ached if he was carrying stuff." Greg wondered if she was paranoid.

"And when he came in, he didn't peer into that mirror in the hall like he always does and ask me if he's looking good."

Norman laughed. "You should be glad. The lad's too conceited by half!"

Maggie ignored this. "And he looked scruffy, as if he hadn't washed. And his clothes were crumpled as if he'd slept in them. Elliot doesn't do scruffy."

"Probably had a night out on the town." Both men smiled knowingly.

"Look, I don't think he drinks much. There's a lot more to it than that." I know you both think I'm bats but there's definitely something going on. Like when we sat down to eat, he patted his lap as if there was a dog waiting to jump up. When he saw me watching, he pretended to brush away something on his jeans."

"So?" Greg couldn't think of an explanation for this other than his wife was deluded.

"So it's all very odd. And earlier on when I wasn't in the room with him, I heard him talking to himself."

"He could take after me on that one. I often talk to myself. Nothing strange in that." Norman was adamant.

"He must have been on his mobile. What did he say?" Greg guessed she would have been listening.

"No, he wasn't on his phone. I thought so at first, but when I went in he was sitting on the sofa smiling, with his arm in that strange stretched-out position again. And anyway I'd already seen his mobile upstairs next to his bed. Well, I didn't hear much, things like … they're not bad as parents go. I've been fortunate. Glad you like them."

Her father chuckled. "They say listeners never hear good of themselves. You were lucky."

"And there was a lot more … something about sharing his bedroom. None of it made sense. It was like he was talking to someone in the room."

"You shouldn't have been listening, Maggie. He wants some privacy when he comes home. I remember when you used to read his diaries. Spying I call it. I hated it when you did that."

"I know and I'm not proud of it. But it's the only way I can find anything out. He never tells me anything."

Greg wasn't leaving it there. "And tonight when you asked him if he had a girlfriend and he said yes he was seeing someone, you wouldn't leave it alone. Talk about the third degree! No wonder he clammed up."

Norman nodded. "Well, if that's all there is, Maggie, it seems a bit trivial to me. We know the girl's name is Maria and that's about it. If he hasn't known her long, he'll bring her home when he's good and ready. He's a good-looking boy. There's probably a whole string of them, lucky devil!"

"There's something else." Maggie's chin stuck out as if she'd left the best to last. "I reminded him that he'd asked to borrow twenty pounds. I actually offered him fifty and he turned it down ... said he didn't need it!"

Norman and Greg suddenly sat up in their armchairs.

"My God he has changed!" Greg whistled through his teeth. "Last time he was here he asked me if he could borrow some money for a car. The time before he asked me to pay the arrears on his rent which I have to say were outrageously high. He's always after money. Always trying it on. This is seriously unlike him."

"And I always give him money when I see him. He seems to expect it, a sort of unspoken tradition. I was going to tell him about that little windfall I've had. Got a bit of cash for him. Bet he won't turn that down! I'll see what happens this time," added Norman.

"Thanks Dad." Maggie nudged Greg. "Come on, let's go to bed. Leave Dad to have a chat with Elliot. He's more likely to talk to him."

It was about ten minutes later that Norman heard Elliot's key in the lock.

*

"Oh, hi Grandad! All on your own?" Elliot came in dripping wet.

"Yes. Your Mum and Dad decided to have an early night." Norman couldn't remember ever seeing him so cheerful.

"Not like them when their only son and heir is visiting," he laughed.

"No."

72

"Fancy a hot chocolate, Grandad?"

"Please. Want me to make it? Don't you want to dry off?"

"No, I'll be fine." Elliot went off to make it, humming to himself.

Norman could hear him talking in the kitchen. Could Maggie have been right?

Two mugs of steaming chocolate and some shortbread biscuits were brought in on a tray. Elliot had a towel over his shoulder and proceeded to sit down and rub his hair dry.

"Come on, Maria. Relax and sit down. I'm going to tell Grandad about you."

"Do you think that's wise?" She curled up next to Elliot.

"I can't keep you to myself any longer." Elliot threw the towel onto the floor.

Norman stirred his chocolate vigorously as he watched his grandson talking to himself. The lad was obviously away with the fairies and yet ... he sat in silence. He wasn't going to comment.

"You must think I'm mad." Elliot saw his grandfather shifting uncomfortably on his chair. Norman was silent.

"I'm not talking to myself if that's what you think. There's more to it than that. Do you believe in the spirit world?"

So that was it! Norman smiled. "Well I always talk to your grandmother when I go to the grave. I suppose I must want to believe it. I like to think she can hear me."

"Good. You see, I've got Maria here with me. This is the girl I told you I was seeing. The trouble is no one else can ... see her I mean. She's a Lost Soul. That's her official title, not ghost. She's sitting here next to me."

"Well, maybe the best thing you can do is tell me all about it." Norman tried not to sound too sceptical.

It must have been an hour later that Elliot finished the story of Mary Makepeace. Maria had nodded quietly throughout.

"But you didn't tell him how ugly I am," she finally said.

"It's not relevant," Elliot told her. She shook her head.

Norman reached for a biscuit and crunched it noisily. Of course he didn't believe this wild story. Elliot had always been imaginative, right from childhood, seemed to live in a world of his own, always had his head buried in a book.

"So, what do you think, Grandad?" Elliot sounded hopeful.

"It's difficult for me. You must know that. But I'm glad you shared the story. You believe it and that's all that matters." Norman fiddled with his mug. He looked at the clock. Past midnight. Past his bedtime.

"No, it's not all that matters." Elliot wasn't going to admit defeat. "I know, I'll prove it to you. Now then I'm going to pass this spoon to Maria and you will see something strange happen. Watch!"

Norman looked across as Elliot appeared to pass the spoon to the empty space next to him. It fell to the ground.

"Maria, why didn't you take it?" Elliot picked up the spoon in disbelief.

"I tried to but I couldn't. I can't do tricks to order. I'm sorry. My actions have to be spontaneous. They have to come out of my own mind you see."

Wearily Elliot relayed that message to Norman.

"I understand," he said. But he didn't. Now he was even more convinced it was all in his grandson's head. Best to go along with it though.

"You won't tell Mum and Dad any of this, will you?"

"Not if you don't want me to."

"I don't. Come on Maria, time for bed." At least he'd got that experience to look forward to. "I've kept Grandad up long enough."

"Good night then … er … both." Norman watched as Elliot stood up and walked to the door.

"See you in the morning, Grandad. Sorry for bending your ear."

"No problem." Elliot went out and Norman stood up and stretched himself. His knees ached after sitting for so long. He suddenly remembered he hadn't told Elliot he had a thousand pounds for him. Maggie would be on to him first thing in the morning about that. Oh well! Tomorrow is another day, he thought.

It was at that moment that the door opened and he felt a slight draught. The towel immediately appeared to rise from where Elliot had left it and floated like a white cloud out of the room.

*

Elliot sat on his bed, waiting. Hopefully Maria hadn't disappeared on him again. Then in she came, carrying the damp towel.

"Maria, did Grandad see you pick up the towel?"

"Yes, I'm sure he did."

"And?"

"I didn't see his reaction. I left quickly to come to you."

"Why did you go back for the towel in the first place?"

"I wanted him to believe you. He needed some proof. Now he knows you are not hallucinating."

"That was sweet of you." Elliot took her in his arms. "And now I'm going to make love to you."

He'd been thinking about it all day and he knew this was the moment. They'd talked about it on the rainy walk that evening.

"Do I need to take precautions?" he'd asked her. It had all seemed so clinical at the time but he wanted to take care of her.

She'd laughed. "A Lost Soul can't produce babies."

The thin lips had curved upwards for a moment and then her head had drooped and she'd suddenly seemed sad.

He slipped the flowery dress over her head, revealing two tiny mottled breasts and a bony, hairless, child-like body. Maria appeared to ignore her nakedness. She looked about her.

"Is this the room you slept in as a boy?"

"Yes. My mother has virtually left it untouched since I went away to uni." Why was she talking about the room at a time like this? Delaying tactics? She knew what was about to happen and he thought she wanted it too.

"You have so many books. It is like a library in here."

"Yes." He ran his fingers through the chestnut hair. "But I want to concentrate on you, darling Maria. Let's forget our surroundings."

She looked up at him anxiously as he lifted her up gently and laid her on the bed. Then he took off his own clothes. For a moment he stood gazing at the small girl lying there, so vulnerable. He wanted everything to be splendid. Maria looked up at him.

"Your body is perfect," she told him. "You have no blemishes anywhere, unlike me."

He put a finger on the thin lips. "Sh! This is not about me. This is about us. I love you Maria."

There, he'd said what he may have said to others in the past, empty words then, but this time he meant it. He bent over her and kissed the thin rubbery lips. They tasted sweet, like ripe strawberries.

And then … an explosion in his head seemed to send the room swirling round as if he were on a fairground ride. He stumbled to his feet.

"Maria!" Where was she? He suddenly saw her standing by the window with her back to him. She was silhouetted against the first morning light. He saw she was wearing a floor-length dress with puffed sleeves and a lacy bonnet.

"Maria!"

She turned round and as her face came into focus, his body began to tremble violently. The lips were full and red and the eyes wide beneath long lashes. Pink cheeks were clearly visible on the clearest of skin. Her bonnet tied with ribbons framed her face like a halo. She held out a gloved hand to him and drew him towards her, still keeping him at arm's length. He could see she was crying.

"Maria, what has happened? Why are you dressed like this?"

"It is quite simple, Elliot. My soul has been saved by you."

"By me?"

"Of course. When you kissed me and you told me you loved me, I was released. You see me now as I once was. The search is ended because my spirit has been finally freed."

"But why are you crying, Maria? Surely this is wonderful news."

"It is what I was compelled to do. It is my destiny. As I have told you before, I don't have complete control over my actions. I was forced to travel through the ages trying to find someone who would love me for myself. You are that person, Elliot."

He knew it was true but he was confused. She looked devastated.

"I am crying because you and I must part and I have grown to love you too. Never forget that. Already I can feel the earthly strength ebbing away and my spirit taking over. This must be goodbye, Elliot. There is no time left now."

"Maria! No!" He moved closer.

She held out her hand to stop him coming further. Her voice grew fainter. "I'm not Maria any more. Mary Makepeace is my name now."

He sank to his knees as he realised she had gone and he could only see the colours of sunrise through the window.

Guilty Secret
Graham Bird

Sandie stepped out of the taxi and stared up at the college entrance, the same dull grey walls and black gates. It had been twenty years and she felt breathless, her heart pounding. So much had happened since that weekend but it was still there every day, an unfaded memory like a repeating movie playing in a corner of her mind.

She'd stayed in his room, a three-day lock-in. She had told her parents the trains were cancelled and she would stay with a friend. There was some truth in it. There were trees down.

Sandie smiled and shivered, pulling her coat a little tighter.

"I can't believe I'm actually going to do this. Mick will be different. After all this time, let's hope we can laugh about 'it'."

The party had started on the Friday night and Sandie and her friends had a special invite from someone in the pub. Mick was just standing in the corner with a group of friends. Sandie blushed at the thought of how wild she had been. Mick and his friends were all that bit older and she'd wanted to impress. She chatted to them all but kept her eyes on Mick.

"Do you know Mick well, then?" Sandie asked one of the girls in the group.

"He's on the same course as me, Political History."

"I bet he's got lots of friends."

"He has, but no-one special." That was it really, all the encouragement needed.

She and Mick had not spoken since that time. She couldn't face that. His email had arrived from nowhere, a sharp stab at her twinge of guilt. She'd used the site to search for her old school-year, a possible reunion of The Smiths fan-club. Sandie and her sister had been founder members. She hadn't wanted to find Mick, that's for sure. But he hadn't forgotten her. And people were starting to put yearbook pictures on the site, so she knew it was only a matter of time before he began to wonder.

For a week she ignored the mail, and then another one came:

Dear Sandie,
I do hope we can at least say hello. You must be 40 this year although you probably don't want me to say that!! I was 42 last week. Time is relentless. But I remember your dark brown eyes, they still smile at me every day. I'm always reminded of that special time whenever they talk of the storm of 1987. You were my storm then.

I hope you'll reply.
Love,
Mick xxx

It was the three kisses that had done it. She was curious. She was sure it would be OK. They could meet somewhere neutral, catch up on twenty years, steer away from difficulties. Why not?

Her daughter Holly was surprised.

"Mum, is that another new dress? Wow, and those heels!"

"Thanks. Well, I have an appointment in Oxford. I may be late home."

Sandie knew that Holly's interest would be short-lived, and she escaped to catch the 9 o'clock train.

Sandie crossed the narrow street to the front door of the club, recognising the former Taj Mahal immediately. She could still see some small lines of the original gold paint in the corner of the doorway. Mick had emailed to meet there as it seemed appropriate, and he said he was a member now. They'd eaten there every day that weekend, the closest and most romantic spot they could find. He said that this Taj Mahal would stand forever like a shining beacon of his love for her. An enduring love. Now, the clean fresh doorway announced the QI Club and she could no longer smell the spices.

Sandie stood tall and smoothed her hair, brushing it behind her ears with her fingers. She'd spent two hours yesterday trying to decide how to look and what to wear. She knew she couldn't recreate a look from that far back, but eventually she found the dangly earrings and gold choker necklace her sister had given her, like symbols of a shared guilty secret. She'd also spent another hour this morning getting ready, hiding the years in her face and experimenting with her eighties style makeup again. The Smiths had so much to answer for.

"Now, come on. Let's get on with this." Sandie strode in through the front door, passing the book shop and upstairs into the dark and intimate bar at the back.

"Oh my god! Sandie!" Mick leapt from his seat and rushed toward her, wrapping his arms around her waist before she could even focus.

"Mick! It's you, it really is you." She kissed him gently on the cheek and extracted herself from his grasp so as to see him better. Mick was the same, standing tall with thick dark brown hair, straggly and uncombed, and sharp blue eyes. His face was alight.

"Let's sit here and order some food." Mick pulled her down beside him, clutching her hand and grinning.

"Mick, it's just amazing to see you after all this time. I can't believe it. I didn't think you'd remember. You went abroad didn't you?"

"Yes, Peru then Bolivia. I was there for five years altogether. It was fantastic, but you never wrote!"

Sandie smiled and pulled her hand from his grasp. "No, but neither did you! I cried for a whole week."

"Communication was so difficult. Then, after a while … well, I assumed you'd have found someone," he said.

Sandie leaned forward. "It's so good to see you. I did meet someone, of course. But that was much later. We divorced last year."

"I'm sorry. What about children? I bet you have beautiful girls."

"Well, I do have one. Holly. What about you?" she asked.

"Well, after five years abroad, I returned to Oxford. It was the early 90's recession. I got a job lecturing in South American studies and I've been doing that ever since. No hidden wife or children. They always seemed to be lower down the list somehow."

Sandie watched as Mick looked through the wine list; he was charming, and she warmed to him. She wanted the hurricane to return, an excuse to stay. She knew she had to tell him eventually, but maybe not today. She felt her resolve fade. It had only meant to be a joke, a student prank. She felt silly now.

The waitress brought two glasses of water and Mick ordered white wine. He'd remembered, she thought.

Mick looked across at her. "So, what have you been doing all these years?"

"Oh, I work in interior design. I was always a bit arty, I guess. I have a small office attached to my house in Chelsea."

Gulping down the water, Sandie bit her lip. "Mick, look, there's something you need to know. Something I should have written to you about all those years ago, or told you about. We shouldn't have done it. I wasn't completely honest at the time."

Mick took her hand again and held it close to his chest.

"Look, Sandie, feel that. My heart is racing just sitting here with you. That's enough for me to be happy." He kissed her on the cheek.

Sandie drew a deep breath. "Do you remember that Sunday morning? The storm was already starting; we couldn't sleep, even though we'd been awake most of the night. The wind was howling, tiles coming off the college roof and falling past your window, crashing on the paving slabs. It was pretty scary really. I was restless and slipped out of bed and put on some clothes."

"I vaguely remember. Certainly watching you dress." He grinned. "You wanted to go and explore and you were gone ages and I got a bit worried. Did I shout at you when you got back?"

"I ... I don't remember."

Deep down Sandie felt embarrassed. But why should she? After all, he hadn't bothered until now, and it was only a bit of fun. He couldn't have missed her that much. A soft smell of spice filled the air, as if the restaurant had never closed. Their restaurant. She was hungry.

The waitress put a hotpot in front of her, and fishcakes for Mick.

"I love hotpot on a day like today," she said.

"I remember your eating! My god, how do you do it Sandie! Look at you, still a great figure. You look wonderful. But I seem to remember you didn't like meat."

Sandie grinned. "Mandy is the vegetarian in our family."

"Who's Mandy?"

"She ... well, she's my sister."

Mick smiled. "Is that right? Oh my! You have a sister too. Well, she'll be gorgeous no doubt. You never mentioned her."

"Mick, there's something you really must know. I ... I need to tell you why I behaved strangely on that Sunday morning. The passion of the weekend drove me to it, I suppose."

"What do you mean, 'behaved strangely'?"

"When I ventured out that Sunday for some milk and a paper, I took your keys from your jacket to let myself back in. I wanted to surprise you with some breakfast. There were branches in the street, stuff flying everywhere. I could hardly stand. I wrapped your scarf round my neck and held my hand up to protect my face from the flying debris. There weren't many people around. I remember passing a vagrant in the entrance to the Taj Mahal, then, as I turned into Broad Street, I saw Mandy. I couldn't believe it, there she was straight in front of me. She'd driven down to my friend's house to pick me up because of the storm."

"So, you could have at least introduced me!"

"Yes, well, anyway, we went for a coffee and I told her all about the party and you. She got all excited and demanded to meet you. Well, we'd done lots of crazy things as kids and always shared everything. But I guess, never anything that crazy."

Sandie sipped some water, calmer now. She looked into Mick's eyes and smiled.

"Do you remember me coming back from the shops?"

"Yes, of course I do," he grinned. "You made me scrambled eggs with smoked salmon, then you told me you'd had the best time. We went back to bed for the day."

"And you enjoyed Sunday more than Saturday, did you? Those eggs rather than my bacon sandwich?"

"Well … it's a long time ago, but, well, yes I think I did actually. Oh, I fell in love with you that day. Then you had to go and I gave you that necklace and earrings. You must remember, you're wearing them now."

"Well yes, it is this necklace. But I got it from my sister, my identical twin sister Mandy."

Jim
Margaret Wilcox

He stood on the corner of Turl Street with the wind ruffling his hair, blowing leaves and rubbish round his feet. I had seen him most mornings but never stopped.

"Big Issue?" he asked hesitantly. His holey jumper, worn shirt and baggy trousers seemed unlikely to keep out the early winter cold.

I was very conscious of my new boots, snug coat and gloves so, feeling guilty, I pulled out my purse.

"How much?" I was surprised at the precise charge and pulled the coins out. He took a magazine off those laid over his right arm and handed it to me with his left. I took the magazine and noticed his right hand was withered. He thanked me; at least I think he did. His speech was so slurred it was difficult to understand him. "Drunk," I thought as I hurried to work at the QI Club. I read the recently purchased magazine during my lunch break and was agreeably surprised at the interesting content so I bought a copy the next week.

He started saying "Mornin' " as I passed him on the way to work. Sometimes something else was added. Could it have been "Nice day" or "Isn't it cold"? I just couldn't decipher it.

Christmas came and he sported a red Father Christmas hat and, by then, we were on fairly chatty terms. That is, he said a lot and I made a stab at guessing what he was talking about. I commented on his hat; he said it kept his head warm. I think. I bought a fleece ski-type hat and wrapped it in Christmas paper as a present. He was so excited when I gave it to him he was like a kid feeling the presents under the Christmas tree. He carefully put it away in the shopping bag on wheels that always stood by him.

"Christmas Day," he explained. This brought tears to my eyes so I hurriedly left him. I had a vision of him on Christmas Day waking up in the shop doorway, or wherever he slept and solemnly opening my parcel. After Christmas he wore my hat all the time.

Sometimes I got understanding him very wrong. I was concerned he would be offended when I misunderstood him, but no. He would laugh and try again. It didn't seem to matter to him how many times he tried, with laughter we got there – or nearly – in the end. Once a crowd of Japanese tourists gathered round us as Jim was telling me something. They were attracted by our laughter thinking this was the entertainment for the day. They joined in the laughter and went away with copies of the Big Issue. I'm not sure if they understood what it was all about.

One week in May he wasn't there. He sometimes missed a day if it was raining but that week was the most perfect spring weather. The following Monday he was there.

"Where have you been?" I asked in relief. "Are you all right?" I suddenly realised I cared about what happened to him.

"Gotta flat," he said really clearly.

"You've got your own flat?" I asked, to make really sure.

"Yuss. Two bedrooms. Social got it. Boy'll come summer."

"You've got a son?" I was surprised. I had always assumed as he slept rough he was on his own. There was more to Jim than rough sleeping.

"Is it furnished?"

"Social helping," he said. "So is the Sally Army."

How marvellous these organisations are, the way they help people. Social Services are much maligned. One mistake and a tragic case all over the papers means all the good they do is forgotten.

As the months went by Jim's speech slowly improved so I could understand him a lot of the time. I commented on this and he said,

"Speech Therapy. Worked hard at it."

It certainly had paid off. I congratulated him and his scarred face lit up in a smile. His clothes, too, had improved. Gone were the tatty clothes he once sported and were replaced by new, clean ones that were changed frequently. He kept me updated on the state of his flat and the furniture he had. The washing machine's arrival was a red-letter day. He was so excited.

"It's a proper home now," he told me.

One day in June I caught an earlier bus as I wanted to get home early. Jim wasn't there. I thought he was having a day off but as I walked up Turl Street I saw him, walking with great difficulty pulling the dilapidated shopping bag. I was shocked at the difficulty he had and waited to talk to him. His right leg was nearly as useless as his right arm; the foot dragged at right angles to the other and the side of it was used to take Jim's weight. It took a long time for him to walk down the road. What a struggle it must be for him to carry out any of the everyday tasks I can do without thinking.

"You're early!" he greeted me. "New one out tomorrow."

"Yes, I know," I said. "I just wanted to say hello."

"That's nice." His face lit up. "Must get on. Customers waiting. Takes me so long to get anywhere with this." He indicated his leg.

I smiled and went on to work with a lump in my throat. Fate had dealt him such a rotten hand but he just accepted his lot and got on with life. What set of circumstances put him in this position? Was he born with his disabilities? Did he have an accident? With his scarred face this seemed probable. Speculation ended as I turned in to the QI Club to work.

Spring turned into summer and one day a young lad stood, proudly, by Jim's side.

"My son, Andy." Jim introduced us. Andy solemnly shook my hand as I introduced myself.

"I've never known your name," said Jim. No, I hadn't seen the need to introduce myself to this rough-sleeping drunk at first, but he was a person now, with a story to tell – as are we all. He always greets me by name in the mornings now. Andy obviously adored his father and could understand him better than me. Now the three of us laughed when I couldn't understand Jim.

That summer we were subjected to very heavy thunder showers and it was because of one of these that I got to know about Jim. I rushed out in my lunch break to do some shopping and I was by Jim and Andy when a storm broke.

The hailstones really hurt and there was nowhere to shelter so I grabbed the magazines and Andy and told Jim to follow me. We fell into the door at the QI Club, glad to be out of the hale stones. But Jim wasn't as quick, so he got wettest. My friends provided towels to dry ourselves and hot drinks followed, although Andy asked for a coke. As we sat there, recovering, I took the opportunity to ask Jim what had happened to his arm and leg. He looked pensive so Andy started with Jim adding information he missed.

Apparently Jim was coming home from work fairly late one evening and he was mugged. Not only did they take his money and cards but the beating they gave him took away his self respect and nearly his life. It was twenty weeks before he regained consciousness. Meanwhile his wife, with the young Andy, was told there was little hope he would survive. If he did, he would be a vegetable. With no money to pay the mortgage she returned to her parents and divorced Jim when she met a new dad for Andy. Meanwhile Jim spent a year in hospital and a year or more in aftercare but eventually he had to find somewhere to live. At first he had a bed in a hostel. He found the company of drunks and junkies unpleasant so one summer he slept out. It was as a rough sleeper that he was introduced to the *Big Issue* and, he said, it was a turning point. Earning a little money selling the magazine gave him back his self respect. He felt he could look people in the eye now. The Social Services saw he was helping himself so helped and the Salvation Army's help was also forthcoming. His wife helped where she could and kept Andy updated on his father's progress. She had done a good job because Andy adored his father and was very conscious of the struggle Jim had endured all because of junkies wanting another fix.

Picking Raspberries
Robin Courage

Miles is watching the girl picking broad beans. Her skirt billows around the stems as she reaches the lower pods, tossing them into her basket. The wind bares her thighs. She wears a bandanna to keep the sun off her head. Sometimes Miles can hear her singing across the wind. Miles dreams, unsure of himself. A green woodpecker calls.

Manor Farm sells wholesale as well as PYO. Miles picks what he hopes is enough, wanting to coincide with the girl when she has her basket weighed for her picking payment. So he walks along the rows, judging his speed and angle to meet her. Miles comes up shyly to the desk ahead of the girl and pays. Then she puts her basket on the scales. The part-time undergraduate staff enter 10.3 kg in the book and laugh with her about the PYO punters and their inane questions. She hears them sharing banter about a party the next night.

"I hear you are doing the flowers for the QI Club party, Millie," one of them says. So now Miles knows her name.

"Yes. I'm borrowing Dad's van to take the flowers there in the morning." Millie starts to walk back to the field with her empty basket. On an impulse Miles asks if he could help pick with her. She places her basket on her thigh and looks straight at him. He waits, wondering. He can't help grinning. Her auburn hair nearly reaches her waist. She picks up the strands and waves them over her shoulders. His grin wins.

They talk easily and he finds out that she is the local gamekeeper's daughter. They walk, letting the beans wait. When they enter a row, their bare arms touch. Miles loves the way she shows her figure as she bends amongst the pods. Millie talks about her easy way of life but how she wants to better herself. She cannot help her deep breathing showing as she straightens up to stretch her back, looking at his tousled hair falling over his grinning face.

The next day, Miles calls at the QI Club, using a cup of coffee as an excuse. Walking down to the cellar, he sees Millie working, assembling vases and posies. He watches quietly, unnoticed. Her hands deftly cut the base of stems, mixing the colours, shaking them alive in sprays in various containers. Some stems she sticks into the green oasis to form patterns. Miles admires her skill. She is absorbed and doesn't notice him till he is beside her. After a hug, Millie hands him some vases to carry to the top floor.

Millie is grateful for the help, so she can make the room three floors up shimmer with petals, pollen and colour. Miles finds himself wondering, this girl and her long hair, could she be the one with those wide eyes, frank eyes, sparkling eyes?

"That's done. Would you like a lift in Dad's van? Where shall we go?"

They walk along the river. Some of the Oxford college crews are rowing, scaring ducks and swans. They turn to each other as they go through one of the kissing gates off the towpath but a dog rushes at them playfully. The owner and his wife call the dog away, apologising. Suddenly Miles realises the dog's owner is his dentist so he smiles Hello. The moment has gone.

Miles asks Millie if she would come to the QI party tomorrow night. Millie thinks, in momentary panic, will she fit in, this gamekeeper's daughter? Miles' smile wins again. He will meet her by the Perch Inn and they will walk together into Oxford. He must remember to bring a torch for the walk back across Port Meadow. Some of that pathway over the water is darkly overhung by scrubby trees where the cattle lie.

When they meet by the Perch, they are momentarily shy, almost embarrassed but Miles' smile relaxes them both and they chatter happily as they cross the meadow. Walking into Broad Street, they share the architecture and turn into Turl Street of Morse fame. Millie takes a deep breath as they enter the QI Club. How will she fit in? Miles takes care to lead her so they can mingle and introduces her to his Christchurch friends. Millie is stunning, her open face displaying honesty, fun and integrity. He glows inside at their reaction.

They dance and sometimes swap with others on the floor for fun, always coming back together. One of the Christchurch crowd says they are going down to the Vodka Bar for a drink. There is a Bohemian atmosphere of noisy laughter. They squeeze in.

After a bit they manage to sit side by side in an alcove, shoulders touching, her long hair between them. They talk about their different upbringings, her wildness with nature, his conventional freedom.

The pair return to the dance floor at the top of the building and notice the leaves of the horse chestnut dancing in the street light of Ship Street. Millie breathes deeply again. She could see people admiring her flowers.

A Worcester College boy approaches Millie and, unsure how to handle the situation, she goes off to dance with him. Miles dances with another girl in pique but when he catches Millie's eyes, the two of them laughingly come together again.

Miles takes Millie to some of his friends so they can look after her while he goes to get some drinks. The opportunist Worcester boy drags Millie out for another dance. When Miles returns with the drinks, he sees them dancing happily. Miles' stomach is churning but Millie comes for her drink and dances again with Miles. He suggests they might go now.

Walking back across the meadow in the dark, the pair hold hands, sometimes giggling when Miles pretends to lose her among the bushes, bouncing out like an excited Tigger. When they go through a kissing gate, they do. They both feel that kiss was different to any others before. They don't share that thought then, but that would come later. They are startled by a noise of brushwood moving amongst the bushes. Their backs tingle so they walk on silently. Miles is no longer bouncing along like Tigger. At the top of the arching footbridge over the canal, they lean over looking at the water below. Miles touches her bare arm.

Later, nearly back at the family cottage, Millie asks if he'd like to help her pick raspberries next week, the broad beans would be over.

A couple of days later, they meet at the PYO. They smile as they see each other and hug quietly. She leads the way to a different field this time. They gradually become excited as they chatter, talking about the party at the QI Club, what they have been doing since. Under an oak tree, Miles takes her hands and leans back against the trunk. She feels the bark as she puts her arms around him, pressing, kissing, longing. The oak watches. This time, as he holds her a little away with his hands on her waist, he speaks of the feeling he has when they kiss, not just this time but from the beginning, as being different. She snuggles her face to his and whispers in his ear. A woodpecker laughs nearby so he doesn't hear it all. She won't repeat what she said, looking embarrassed now.

"Come on. Let's pick the raspberries. That's why I've come here."

They enter the rows and pick back to back, sometimes touching as the sun flickers between the tall canes. The red berries twinkle in the shafts of sun. She pops one into his mouth. They laugh and Miles asks her again what it was she said when the woodpecker interrupted her.

"You talked about the feeling being different, from the first time on the way back from the party. That difference is the same for me. I can't explain better than that. I was agreeing with you when the woodpecker interrupted and I wasn't brave enough to say it again but I can now. Kiss me and I'll show you."

They reluctantly pick some more raspberries in their military rows, their breathing heavy. There are voices of other pickers, but in the distance. When they bend down to pick on their opposite rows, their bottoms nudge. They laugh openly and kiss, this time harder, urgently. They fondle and play and whisper, though the raspberries can't hear.

A blackbird startles past them. They fill their baskets, the canes waving goodbye in the wind as they make their way to the PYO weighing machine. The woodpecker laughs again.

Miles takes his gamekeeper's daughter by the hand and they walk down by the river. Along the bank, they catch sight of a tributary, without dogs, people or boats. Millie stops to pick some wild flowers, tying the stems together with a long piece of grass. She tickles Miles' cheek with his posy.

They entwine their fingers, their feet shuffling through the grass, leaving a trail for others to notice and wonder. Later, they lie in the afternoon sun, talking, feeling comfortable together.

"Miles, you've told me about your parents and your sister but I haven't heard anything about your brother."

"Well, where do I start? He and I are very close even though he's six years older than me. We're close because he always seems to be in various scrapes over his women and he talks to me about them in a way he can't to our parents. Hopefully, I may have learned from him some of the pitfalls to avoid."

"Where does he live, Miles?"

"Oh, not far, on a farm outside Horton-cum-Studley."

"So what does he get wrong?"

"Perhaps it's just circumstances or luck," Miles continues. "His last girlfriend was called Sylvia. She was lovely and they adored each other. It really looked as if he had at last met the right one. She did seem a bit strange sometimes but we put that down to the fact that she had recovered from ME and had a terrible childhood which left some scars. We all liked her, Dad particularly as her father had been a gamekeeper too. Anyway, it transpired eventually that Sylvia suffered from Asperger Syndrome. That made her behaviour totally focussed on herself and impossible long-term. I'll tell you more about her another time."

They chatter on, comparing their respective families. Though their upbringings are so different, they do share the familiarity and love of the countryside.

Her knowledge was gleaned from her gamekeeper father and his need to supplement his meagre wages by adding to the family stew pot, in addition to the hares and rabbits he was expected to take. The hares would otherwise decimate the young trees the estate planted regularly. Tree guards were not high enough against a full grown hare standing up on its hind legs, so he would shoot them. The rabbits ate significant amounts of grass, almost twenty metres into the sheep's grazing from the edge of the woods.

His knowledge was from the other side of the blanket, so to say. His father's shoot was well known in Oxfordshire for its high driven birds, the patient waiting beside the ponds for flights of duck against the sky. The firm handling of the Springer Spaniels, curbing their enthusiasm in their zeal to flush game from the bramble thickets, their tails wagging as the dogs bring birds back to their handlers, gruffly praised with a hand smoothing the head, the more gentle Labradors at their best in the open fields putting up a covey of partridge, returning proudly with a bird, dropping one to pick up another perhaps.

Miles' upbringing had been hugely influenced by his father's estate, by the countrymen who would take him aside to show him the spoor of the doe, the slots pointing outwards slightly in the earth. The buck would walk with his slots pointing straight.

As the sun went down, they walked some more along the bank till the stream joined the main river. They disturbed coots and moorhens which would scatter in a panic back into the water. A blackbird sang goodnight as it flew to roost in the hedge. Millie said she should return to her family and so Miles offered to walk her home.

"No, thank you, Miles. I will be fine."

He was unhappy about this but she seemed determined so they parted with a kiss, agreeing to meet the next day on the bridge over the river. Miles made as if to turn towards his college but almost immediately followed Millie surreptitiously. He was not wanting to spy, he just could not risk her falling into trouble. He hadn't disclosed to her he thought they were being followed that first night when he was gambolling like Tigger between the kissing gates on the meadow.

The moon came out which made it easy for him to follow at a safe distance. He had to hide behind a tree when she slowed and went to the edge of the path. Miles chuckled to himself when Millie squatted without a care in the world. Miles was enjoying his game, imagining he was protecting his girl. It doubled his distance to return to his studies but they would be difficult after today's excitement. She was nearly home now, the light from the door opening reassured him and he set off down the path back to Christchurch.

Miles stopped dead and looked behind. He thought he heard a stone. He couldn't see anything. A cloud had chosen that moment to block the moon. He waited against the fence. A break in the clouds let the moon shine again and there was a figure running in the field away from him. Miles shivered and continued on his way. After all, he had seen Millie go into her front door.

A little way along the path his conscience caught up with him and Miles turned back. He stopped by the cottage gate and listened. He could hear raised voices. He opened it gently and crept up to a curtained window. Millie's father was shouting at her but from further inside the cottage so he couldn't hear the words. Miles tiptoed round the wall to be nearer the sounds.

As he turned the corner of the building, he froze. Not two metres from him was a tall man with his ear to the window and his back to him. Miles could hear his own heart pounding. He stepped on a stone which caught the other guy's attention. Their eyes glared and the other man lunged for Miles. As they fought for control, their bodies moved along the wall, grazing themselves on the rough brickwork. Miles found his head being scraped and banged. His adversary leant against the window, breaking a pane.

Now there was bedlam. Millie and her father rushed out of the cottage to find the two men scrabbling on the ground. The gamekeeper hauled the other man from Miles.

Millie was screaming, "Get out of my sight, get out of my sight. You know I don't want to see you."

He left, limping.

"So this must be Miles," the gamekeeper said. "You'd better come in. Millie, ask your mother to clean him up. He's going to make a mess."

Vodka Bar Spirit
Nicola Wilcox

TO THE GLORY OF GOD,
AND IN GRATEFUL COMMEMORATION
OF HIS SERVANTS,
THOMAS CRANMER,
NICHOLAS RIDLEY,
HUGH LATIMER,
PRELATES OF THE CHURCH OF ENGLAND,
WHO NEAR THIS SPOT
YIELDED THEIR BODIES
TO BE BURNED,
BEARING WITNESS
TO THE SACRED TRUTHS
WHICH THEY HAD
AFFIRMED AND MAINTAINED
AGAINST THE ERRORS
OF THE CHURCH OF ROME,
AND REJOICING THAT
TO THEM IT WAS GIVEN
NOT ONLY TO BELIEVE IN CHRIST,
BUT ALSO TO SUFFER FOR HIS SAKE;
THIS MONUMENT WAS ERECTED
BY PUBLIC SUBSCRIPTION
IN THE YEAR OF OUR LORD GOD,
MDCCCXLI.

Anwar stood under the Martyrs' Memorial in St Giles and read the inscription. He often passed it but today, the 21st March, something had made him stop and actually look and, as he read their story, he understood. Looking up he quailed under the stony gaze of the sombre man in the strange hat who loomed above him and looked ready to drop the Holy book on his head. He must hurry; he had an important appointment with the Vodka Bar at the QI Club.

As he entered the bar and ordered an orange juice he was thoughtful. The barman noted the order, but whether he actually took in the small dark man was unlikely. Anwar accepted his drink quietly and went to sit on a white upholstered banquette in the corner. He had chosen the QI Club Vodka Bar as it represented all that was wrong with society. He knew he stuck out; he was the first in so he sat fiddling with his drink and running over and over what he had been told. How he alone could change things.

The elders had made it sound so easy, so right, but somehow now it didn't seem so simple. Or was he weak, a coward? He tucked his bag under his feet, but minutes later decided it would be better by his side. As he lifted it and turned to put his burden on the seat beside him he was startled to find it occupied.

"You don't mind if I sit here, lad?" the old guy croaked, his voice the cracked and dry one of a lifelong smoker.

"If you must." Anwar glanced sourly around the empty bar. 'I'll take this one with me!' he thought.

The newcomer was also out of place. He was old, very old, but sat stiffly upright and wore an extraordinary shapeless robe with a wide scarf and he was clutching a square felt hat. He spoke slowly and carefully with a northern accent. His unusually grizzled beard might have excited comment, but seemed quite normal to Anwar's eyes.

'What was this strange old man doing in a place like this anyway?' Anwar mused. No matter, his mind wandered. Maybe he should get it over with, but he knew it was too soon. The bar would start to fill up later, as groups of loud girls made a night of it.

He was right to wait. Before long a group of girls filtered in, fresh from work judging by the look of their clothes. Anwar looked them up and down taking in the short skirts and aggressively high heels. He frowned in disdain.

Most offensive of all was the bold way each girl scanned the room as she entered. These girls didn't have the shy grace of his Hinna. Only that morning she had whispered to him that she had something to tell him when he came home, but now he would never know. The old man cut across his reveries.

"You come from Oxford?" he asked mildly.

"I'm studying here," Anwar snapped.

"I'm a Cambridge man, though I was born in Nottinghamshire," the old chap wheezed bronchitically. Anwar was amazed at this man's persistence but, they say, know your enemy.

"What did you study?" He may as well find out more.

"My studies were held up by a bit of trouble with a woman." Despite himself Anwar found himself drawn in. Hard to imagine this old guy, smelling so strongly of smoke and fags, in trouble over a girl.

"Several women," he added, somewhat bitterly. "I suppose you could say, though, I was studying the nature of mankind."

"Psychology?" questioned Anwar.

"If this is what you say now," replied the old man, somewhat obtusely. "We would say theology. I'm seeking a greater understanding of my fellow man."

"How so?"

"Take you for instance You're studying to …?"

"It was my dream to come to Oxford to study, better myself."

"Part of a dream to do the best for your family. Eh, Anwar?"

"If that is His will," Anwar agreed, somehow unsurprised to hear his name. "What brought you to Oxford then?"

"My beliefs brought me here, my writings, the many wives and My Lord's divorces. Plus the books I published."

"Books?"

"You won't have read the Book of Common Prayer but it's still used every day!" the old man boasted. "After the divorces I'd upset too many, including the papist bastard. She saw to it I ended up here, quite some time ago."

The old timer rasped on. "The one thing I did learn in my time in Oxford is to stick by your friends, those you really care about, and all that you truly believe in. I made some stupid choices. But only one I really regretted, and I had the brains to put that right in the end," he said rubbing his hand.

"What was that?" Anwar was interested now.

"Oh, affirming transubstantiation, accepting papal supremacy, all that."

Anwar didn't understand what he meant, transub-what? But he understood the feeling. He, too, wanted to change the world. He had been so sure he was doing the right thing. But now he was confused. What if there was a better way? What if he regretted his choice? It would soon be too late to do anything about it. What about Hinna? His wife would be so proud when she heard what he'd done but how would she cope alone? What about the news she hugged to herself?

"Look, I lost a son long ago," the old man continued. "Don't make that mistake, Anwar. You are needed here; your son will need you, your strength and advice if he is to make a difference."

Suddenly Anwar understood everything; this old man could see what others could not, this was how he knew his name.

"My son?" Anwar questioned. The man nodded. Anwar's head was singing. A son! I am to be the father of sons. I will call him Mohammed. I will buy him a red tricycle. He will change the world. I will be there for him. Anwar grinned stupidly and then stood up abruptly, almost knocking the table over.

"I must go now," he said.

The old man smiled his understanding. "Delighted to meet you Anwar. Cranmer's the name." He offered his hand to shake. Anwar reached for it then drew back, the hand was black. Black and wizened. It looked burnt, like charcoal.

"Go in Peace my son," the man said, quietly stroking his long beard as Anwar shot out of the door.

The barman looked up and was surprised to see an empty table in the corner of the buzzing bar. He had noticed the little guy sat apart jabbering to himself, but hadn't seen him leave.

"You know they say this place is haunted 'cos they're the old city walls," he laughed to his colleague. "Seems ole Archbish' Cranmer's seen off another punter."

Some time later two homeless men and a stray dog were the only witnesses as a small, dark and agitated man leant over the parapet of Magdalen Bridge and dropped a bulky rucksack into the Cherwell.

Is disease conquering our conkers?
Liz Henderson

It is summertime but the living is not easy for the horse chestnut tree in Jesus College. Its magnificent canopy towers above the wall on the corner of Ship Street and Turl Street. It has probably been there for 250 years, originally in the stable yard but now in the cycle store for the College. Through the grilled gate on Turl Street, passers-by can see that, although it is mid-summer, the bicycles and ground are scattered with fallen leaves.

Has autumn come early?
Horse chestnut trees throughout the south of England have turned brown very early again, but their dry leaves and early leaf drop are not a sign of the season. They have had to struggle against two enemies. The fungi that cause bleeding cankers (*Phytophthora cactorum & criticola*) exude a black tarry substance, killing the trees only if an entire ring of bark around the trunk is destroyed. The more common and extensive problem is infestation of the leaf-miner moth (*Cameraria ohridella*), so-called because the larvae 'mine' the flesh between the outer layers of the leaves, creating a translucent track behind them. In summer they can hatch two weeks after the eggs have been laid so when it is warm, up to six generations can develop in one summer. There can be as many as 700 leaf-miners on one of the tree's palmate leaves! In the winter the larvae can survive for six to seven months as pupae in dead leaves on the ground. In the spring the moths hatch and live off the fresh young leaves.

Leaf-miner moths are about 5mm long, shiny and striped, with bright-brown wings. They thrive in wet springs and warm summers, like those we have had recently in the UK. Hard winters do not bother them, they have been known to survive temperatures of minus 23 degrees centigrade; that is as cold as the inside of a freezer.

What can we do?
Clearly we all want to find a way to control the leaf-miner moth, but so far there is no perfect answer. Chemical poisons cannot be used in cities or public parks. Biological control has been considered. There are about 15 natural enemies of the moth, most of them parasitic wasps, but none of them seems to be effective as enemies in Britain. The University Parks Department, Oxford City Council and Harcourt Arboretum adopt a 'good hygiene' policy: the fallen leaves are gathered and composted in the

autumn. High temperatures, over 60 degrees centigrade, develop in big compost heaps and this destroys the over-wintering larvae.

How has this problem arrived in Oxford?

It seems likely that our use of wheeled transport has been responsible for the rapid spread of the larvae and the distribution area is widening at a rate of approximately 40 miles a year from the south east, northwards.

The Forestry Commission estimates that one kilogram of over-wintering leaf-litter, which is about half a black sackful of dry leaves, can produce 80,000 eggs by the next spring. It is these fallen leaves that are the means by which the insect population increases.

The trees do not thrive when infested, but few die. Experts believe that horse chestnuts will probably not suffer as the elms did in 1967 when Dutch elm disease destroyed most of the great elms in the UK.

Local Action

Nick Collinson of The Woodland Trust believes that the greatest threat to horse chestnuts nationwide may be the disproportionate response of some local authorities, who over-react for fear of a death from 'Falling-Conker Syndrome' or the more common affliction of court action by the 'Branch-Drop Litigation Brigade'.

Some Local Authorities view trees as expensive threats to the health and safety of local people; this, despite all we know of the benefits trees provide to the environment and the human psyche. Fortunately the combined approach of Oxford's tree wardens is more sanguine. They cannot collect every infested leaf as it falls but have a robust approach to destroying the autumn leaf-fall.

Their responsibilities for the safety of the general public are paramount, but their risk assessments are realistic. Unless there is immediate and serious danger to passers-by or property, they regard the current problems with horse chestnut trees as 'cosmetic'.

The Future

Conkers will continue to fall on Turl Street and elsewhere in Oxford. Our children will collect them, as generations have before them. We will always marvel at the nut's parade-ground polish and the pale, satin-lined cradle within the fiercely armoured case. We can all look forward to Oxford's children enjoying collecting and playing with conkers and if they don't, it will be because of obsessive health and safety issues and not because the leaf-miner moth has played executioner to our trees.

The New Barmaid
Margaret Wilcox

Liz walked round the small bar straightening the chairs and collecting the odd stray glass. She was so glad to have got this job; it would help with her finances while she was at uni. Suddenly she realised there was someone sitting at the table in the corner.

"I'm sorry, I didn't see you come in. It's very dark here. The bulb must have gone."

"It's quite alright, young maid. I prefer the softer light of times past than the hard bright light of now."

Liz was surprised at how old he looked to be in a bar mainly frequented by students and teenagers.

"Can I get you a drink?"

"No, I thank you."

Not only did he have an unusual way of speaking, his voice was rough like a long time smoker. Liz went back to the counter and checked that everything was organised. She had done bar work before but that was in a busy bar in her home town. There she had met lots of people and made lots of friends. Here, though, it was different. The bar was small and the only spirit they served was vodka. There was a cold feel about it as well but, she knew it would get warmer when it filled up. If it got busy, that is. The manager was nice and helpful and, to her relief, he left her to work on her own. He said he was in the office, and if she needed him, just to ring.

Raymond came down the stairs and gave her a quick peck on the cheek.

"How's it going, Doll?" he enquired. She was glad to see her boyfriend because she was bored.

"Well, it's a bit quiet. No one has come in except that old man over there and he's not drinking. I haven't poured a drink yet."

"Which old man?" enquired Raymond.

"Over there," said Liz turning to the corner. "Oh, he's gone."

"I expect it's the Archbishop's ghost," Raymond said laughing. "He's been seen down here."

"You're just trying to frighten me. Well, it won't work," Liz laughed at him. "I bet he's gone to the loo. You know what these old boys are like with their bladders."

"I'm not trying to frighten you," Raymond protested. "There have been stories that he has been seen down here. That wall over there is part of the old town walls. Archbishop Cranmer fell out with the Queen and she had him burnt at the stake near here."

"I don't believe in ghosts, so you won't frighten me," Liz retorted sharply.

Raymond said she should start serving drinks with a large one for him. Liz turned to the optics and put a double in the glass.

"That's a bit mean," Raymond said indignantly. When Liz protested he said, "They won't miss it. Anyway they can afford it." Liz was very unhappy about this but she gave him the drink, which he swallowed in one gulp. Liz was concerned that he seemed to drink rather a lot. That bothered her.

"I've got to go, Doll," said Raymond. "I'll pick you up after work and we'll go back to my place." Liz didn't want this. Not tonight. But she decided to leave the arguing until after work.

Looking round, she suddenly realised that the old boy was back. Liz went over to him and the smell of smoke hit her as she neared the table. That is what he had been doing, thought Liz.

"I didn't see you come back." Liz suddenly saw there was ash on the table and felt very cross. "You've got ash all over the table. Don't you know that there is a smoking ban? There is a large fine if you smoke inside, that is, here or the toilets." Liz collected a cloth and cleaned the table.

"I've always been in trouble," the old man muttered. "The ladies have been my undoing. In fact, one saw the end of me. That is of no consequence. I've come today to see you don't take a wrong turn, Liz. I had children that I never should have had but was never around to help them. I want to help you."

Liz felt uneasy; how did he know her name? She asked him what he was talking about.

"My troubles are of no consequence and were over many years ago. Yours are about to start if you don't stop and take the right path. Listen to your friends and your own heart. Do not be swayed from the difficult path you must take. It won't be the easiest path but take it you must if you want happiness and not misery with that young man."

Liz was very perturbed and asked him what he was talking about.

"I think you understand. Take it from someone who has made many mistakes because I did not take the harder path. Instead I went the easiest way and had many ladies that I should never have even looked at. Please, I beg you, don't make the same mistakes, but take the harder path."

Confused, Liz walked back to the bar saying, "How do you know about me?" She turned to the table in the corner waiting for an answer but the chair was empty. Her legs were decidedly wobbly so she sat in the nearest chair.

"Come on lads. The Vodka Bar is empty and the new barmaid needs some work to do." Six students poured in and sat round a table and a shaken Liz got up to serve them.

"At least I know what to say to Raymond tonight," she thought.

Stitched in time
Dion Vicars

'If I could be with you
One hour tonight
De dum de-dum de-dummmm...'

Belinda had always known the King was singing that song to her alone. They had suffered the pain of separation all through the thirty-one years but loving Elvis had given her the strength for each new day. Tonight was the time of his coming though; the calculations given in the Elvis.org website had been consistently correct, the site filled with facts and predictions.

The astro-mathematics were impeccable. In the late seventies, following His departure, the Weisenberg time tunnel effect had been discovered and the mathematics refined. The start is anchored in space and time by an intense event but the end of the tunnel is free to roam in hyperdynamic space, like a whirlwind, searching for the right circumstances to re-attach itself to what we call the real world.

Belinda had set up the model of Gracelands down to the last minute detail at exactly 3.1415% of the original under the Turl Street window of her room in Jesus College. The Grecian Doric columns, the Appolonian pediment, the timeless Vase all perfectly modelled at a scale reflecting the dilation of the time tunnel, thereby creating the resonance needed to attract it.

Tonight at 2 a.m. would be the time of His coming when this room will be at precisely the same point in physical galactic space that Gracelands had occupied 31 years 5 months 17 days and 2 hours ago when He passed into hyperdynamic space.

Since then Belinda had played the sacred record 31,414 times; this last playing would complete the cycle and they would be together at last. She sensed, too, His impatience for their hour. But first there is to be a sign from the radio. She turns it on.

"Good morning listeners, this is BBC Radio 3 on 91.7 megahertz and the time is 1.59 a.m. The news will follow shortly, but in the meantime please take a few moments to move your clocks forward one hour to herald the start of British summer time."

Beep, beep, beep, beep, beep, beeeeeep.

Tamara's Solution
Isabel James

Tamara placed her well-shaped behind on the aluminium chair outside the Broad Street coffee shop.

"I am going to quit smoking", she said, flung back her head and inhaled her cigarette deeply as if to make the most of the nicotine.

"Really?" her friend Felicity said, taken aback.

"Well, I've got one cigarette left after this one," Tamara explained, blowing out the smoke through her plump, red lipsticked mouth. "The thing is, I need every penny I can get. I can't continue to live on pot noodles. Every time I need a cigarette I'll look at my bank balance."

So far, the only thing Tamara had done with the bank statements that came through the letterbox was throw them unopened on a pile in the corner of her bedroom. '*What I don't see doesn't exist*' was her motto.

"The thing is, it is so hard to give up smoking," Tamara said.

"What about nicotine patches?" Felicity suggested.

"I've tried that. The problem is, I get addicted to nicotine patches."

"You don't."

"I do. Besides, they look ugly when I wear my sleeveless tops."

"You're always full of excuses." Felicity shook her head but could not help smiling.

"If I can delay paying the rent until next month I'm okay because then the student loan will come through," Tamara continued.

"You'll just have to sweet talk the landlord," Felicity said. "Make sure you wear a low-cut top when you see him. Why don't you go home? Your parents have got plenty of dosh, haven't they?"

"They have but the old man has decided to do some 'tough love' on me. Says I've got to stand on my own two feet." Tamara had always counted on being Daddy's little girl.

"So the money has well and truly dried up then?" Felicity asked.

"Yep, you could say that. I've spent about £100 on going to London." Felicity looked puzzled.

"I know what I can do: get a credit card!"

"That's a bad idea," Felicity said and they both laughed. Then Felicity had an idea:

"When it gets to August, can't we extend our overdraft?"

"I've already done that," Tamara replied. "I don't want more money I am going to spend on consumer gadgets."

"Yeah, like that iPod you got last week," Felicity recalled.

Tamara's pretty face scrunched up in a frown. "I know, I know. My bank account is suffering for it." How she loved her iPod. She took it everywhere, jogging, lectures … She went silent for a minute, very unusual for her, and then said,

"I am going to have to get my job back. If I work in a bar that's 20 quid a week."

"What happened to your last job at the Vodka Bar?" Felicity asked.

"It's a long story." Tamara looked embarrassed.

"Do you remember what I told you about the casinos?" asked Felicity.

"I don't know much about gambling but I know it's good if you want money quick. If I remember correctly you said, if you gamble double on Roulette you can't lose."

"Yes, you can," Felicity said.

"Anyway, I am not doing anything illegal," Tamara asserted.

"What you need is a rich boyfriend to bankroll your lifestyle," Felicity suggested.

"There are not enough men in Oxford. Maybe my expectations are too high."

"There are plenty of men in Oxford, they're just not stupid enough to get involved with you. You're only after one thing."

"Yes, money!" Tamara threw back her long hair and laughed. "I think blackmail and prostitution are the best ways to make money. It would be easier to sell myself."

"You're not serious are you?" Felicity asked. Tamara went silent.

"What about that guy you met in the Kings Arms a while ago?" Felicity asked.

"Which one?"

"The Brad Pitt look-alike," Felicity reminded her.

"He was cute but penniless."

"And then there was that older guy who chatted you up when you were working behind the bar."

"Who?"

"The suave one with the expensive wrist watch. He looked a bit like Pierce Brosnan," Felicity added.

"Ah, Alex. I was very drunk. I can vaguely remember stumbling down Turl Street trying to find my way home."

"Alex would make sure your financial side is taken care off. How old is he, 35?" Felicity asked.

"About 39. That's it! I could be his classic girlfriend." Just then

Tamara's mobile phone rang.

"Hello. ... Yes, that's right. ... What am I wearing? Can you call me back this evening please?"

"Who was that?" Felicity asked.

"My first customer," Tamara replied.

"You're joking aren't you?" Felicity asked but Tamara did not reply. Instead, she put her mobile back into her handbag, stood up and said:

"Let's go back to college and have that last cigarette."

Conkers
Liz Henderson

The Larson cartoon made Catherine smile, the first smile for a long time. The drawing showed a worried-looking man, rummaging down the back of a sofa. *'Gilbert was looking for his purpose,'* the caption read.

That was it. She'd lost her *purpose*. Oscar's death last year had left her lost and lonely at only 45. He had been such good company, a true soulmate. Time passed slowly now without him; she was still living one day at a time and knew she needed something to absorb and interest her. Muttering to herself, she looked out of the window of her little town house.

"I could learn to draw, maybe I have some of mother's talent." She looked again at a small portrait hanging beside her. "Mmm, that's a place to begin, something completely new; drawing."

The monotone works in the gallery later that day suited her mood. Her lips moved silently as she read each label. Sinking onto the bench in the middle of the room she flicked through the catalogue, her nervous fingers bothered the corners of the pages. She wished she had known her mother; that *Ayleen Sommers* who had written neatly in the corner of the framed works that hung at home. Maybe she had passed on some of her artistic ability to Catherine.

An elderly man was standing nearby. Still tall despite his age, he stooped occasionally to peer over his large glasses to examine a picture more closely, screwing up his eyes and furrowing his cheeks. His loose tweed jacket hung in an untidy fold from his back, disturbing the lines of the weave, accentuating rounded shoulders and craning neck muscles. Huge ears supported hearing aids but when he moved his strides were long. With some embarrassment he gave her a quick smile as he brushed against her foot.

"Sorry. Not looking where I was going." The cultured voice was loud, people turned to look. Catherine stood up and approached a delicate pastel drawing of a baby.

"That is such a beautiful one, isn't it?" she said to him.

"Mmm. Not my favourite though, a bit over-worked."

He stepped back from a bold image of a girl; a slight smile, almost of recognition, crossed his face. From his inside pocket, he took out a black note-book and a fountain pen. Holding the pen loosely, far from the nib and standing firmly, he began to sketch the outlines of her energetic young face, framed as it was by a patterned straw hat. She was laughing as she unfurled an umbrella, its scalloped edge repeating the irregular curve of her hat's brim. He looked at the image for a long time, rapt and intense, unaware of Catherine's manoeuvres behind him. Over his shoulder she could see a skilful outline that captured the movement of the girl's head as it looked up, smiling.

In the café later he hovered with a tray.

"Do you mind?" he said.

"Of course not, please."

"Good show, don't you think?" He smiled quickly before patting his jacket pockets. "Damn. I think I've lost my pen, it must be in here somewhere."

He grunted as he emptied his pockets, spreading the contents on the table. She tried not to look.

"I don't need half of this stuff." He brought out another handful and laughed. "There it is. But look at this conker – I picked it up on my way here. Aren't they perfect when they are newly out of their cases?"

"Yes, beautiful. In our day we were allowed to play 'conkers' at school," she said. "I remember always beating my friend; she was a poor loser, used her conker as a weapon sometimes."

He smiled and said, "We used to hide behind the hedge and throw conkers at cars down in the lane." His eyes twinkled and she could almost see him as a child.

"Oh no." Catherine laughed.

"One day our poor Nanny had an irate driver at the door. My brothers and I were off like greased lightening; hid in the bamboo behind the pond. But …well … that's history. Anyway what brought you to Dulwich today? The Trustees here seem to think people come mainly for this excellent café."

He explained that he had been a Trustee for two years and they chatted about the history of the Gallery. She confided in him briefly about her artistic mother who had died young, leaving her as a toddler.

"Was there a portrait in there that you especially liked?" he said as he bent to drink his tea.

"Not really; although the girl with the umbrella was lively." Her quick answer sounded ignorant and weak.

"Yes, that one is really fine – done by one of Stanley Spencer's contemporaries you know."

Catherine nodded ... who? He picked up the conker and rolled it in his large hand, his long fingers curling and caressing the polished surface.

"It was a conker like this one that changed my life. Odd how these memories get triggered."

"Changed your life?"

"Set me off on drawing, I mean. One day, I was in Oxford. Do you know Turl Street there?

"Yes."

"There's a horse chestnut tree that hangs over a wall. I bent down to pick up a huge conker, like this one. Its case was just splitting, I could see the dark varnished conker inside and when I split it open I felt the smooth dampness of the case. I was in the middle of the road, not expecting any traffic and not looking where I was going. Suddenly, crash! A young woman on a bike ran into me."

"Were you hurt?"

"Not really, but by Jove she was furious. I took her into a coffee bar on the corner to try to calm her down. When she heard I was in the road picking up a splendid conker, she stopped ranting, stared at me and suddenly laughed."

"That was good of her."

"Yes. We got to know each other a bit before she moved away. She was an art student. Later she showed me how to draw, so *she* started me off."

"Bit of a lucky accident then."

"Mmm," his grey gaze settled on the lawn outside. "She left Oxford after a few months."

"Did you ever see her again?"

"No. It was a pity. We swapped drawings the day she left and that was the end of it. I've still got hers. Actually, that drawing of the girl with the umbrella; it reminded me of her ... something about the eyes I think."

"What did you give *her*?"

"Huh." He lifted his eyebrows at the memory. "One of my first drawings. A poor pencil sketch of that beautiful conker; the one I had found in Turl Street." He returned to his tea with a smile.

Catherine ambled back through the shallow tide of leaves on the pavement. One of those warm accessible people with whom it was easy to talk of personal things, she thought. She stopped at the art shop and, equipped with a small sketch book and a selection of pencils, wandered back towards the station. As she passed a horse chestnut tree she picked up one of the unopened cases. She turned its spiky form in her hand, looking for the seam along which it was nearly splitting. Inside she could imagine the glossy conker, shrouded in the silken white security of its protecting armour. She'd have a try, got to start somewhere, but sitting on a park bench, it was hard to know where to begin. Should she look at the whole thing, outline its rounded shape and then add the spikes, or work her way round, drawing the tiny peaks one at a time? Her efforts were childish and clumsy. She needed a rubber. Back in the shop, as she was paying the assistant, she saw another conker, lying beside the till.

"An old gentleman left it here just now. He'd mislaid his keys and took it out of his pocket while he was looking for them," said the assistant.

"Which way did he go?" Catherine asked. "I'd like to talk to him. I know him."

"He's only just gone. I think he went into the park."

Darting about along the paths and through the trees, she strained for a glimpse of him, on a bench or striding on the paths. Eventually she abandoned the search and walked slowly back to the station. Silly. She was getting, what her daughter would have called 'sad'. A lonely middle-aged woman who imagined friendships with passing strangers. On the platform she shuddered and wrapped her jacket around her. In the train she leaned back and was sorry she had let a chance go by. He was interesting and she might have learned how to draw, with his help.

At home she walked around with a mug in her hand, marvelling anew at her mother's drawings, appreciating their skill and sensitivity more than ever. In the attic she knelt to spread out the portfolio. One by one she examined the drawings, absorbed by each one's subtlety. After her infantile efforts that afternoon she looked in a different way. More appreciative and with more understanding. Catherine turned the pages, enjoying the originality of each one, loving the closeness she suddenly felt for her mother.

Her quiet gasp disturbed the silence as she looked at the last sheet. It was small and slightly yellowing; drawn on cheaper paper perhaps. A weak flat image that might have been drawn by a child. The pencilled conker floated, unsupported, in the middle of the page. She sat back on her heels and held it closer. It was not her mother's work. It lacked the strong lines and had no depth. Lost in recalling the story of the young man crouching in the middle of Turl Street, she was glad she had this pencil sketch to remind her; a pity she had no way to get in touch with him. She replaced the drawing, but as she did so, turned it over. There was a faded inscription on the back. She whispered aloud,

'To Ayleen. Thanks for good times and here's to future success. Patrick Cobden.'

A Quite Interesting Corner
Birte Milne

QI for the curious with an above average IQ. Not the MENSA type candidate, but rather your investigative, interested in everything informative and trivial, type of person. Curiosity killed the cat, however, quite interestingly, the QI is not in Catte Street, but located in a Georgian building on the corner of Turl Street and Ship Street.

Built in 1785 by a Mr Priddy, who no doubt would have found it quite, if not extremely interesting, had he known, that during the next 200 years his corner edifice was to graduate from student accommodation and coffee house to Oxford's very own Taj Mahal.

Here, in a quiet corner, many a student has pondered over textbooks and essays, while trying to keep his thoughts from drifting away on a curried cloud towards other quite or more interesting topics. Sustained and fortified by the curious culinary creations of the Bahadur brothers, the revision stamina and pass rates must have reached unprecedented levels between 1945 and 1992.

The Quite Interesting has now become The Corner. We must wait and see if it still remains: A Quite Interesting Corner.

The Authors

"Stranger than fiction." This is how **Birte Milne** describes her life since leaving Denmark in 1981. Once a teacher, now a school librarian and 'host mother', she has seen it all. "You just couldn't make it up if you tried," she says. Her writing draws on her experiences and the people she has been lucky enough to come across. She has had several plays performed and short stories published. She is currently working on her first novel.

Dion Vicars was unable to spell or write at school and wisely moved into maths and computing where he honed his skills producing documentation and reports. As a teacher he progressed to course notes and a few academic papers, but has since found that making it up is more fun. All this is an excellent background for the fabrication of pseudo-science. He is curious and amused by the way social systems and technology affect lives.

Graham Bird started writing fiction in 2004, creating a number of short stories and a novel. He loves to develop complex mystery characters in everyday settings, drawing on his experiences in business and travelling.

Isabel James has lived in Oxford for 13 years. She co-performed her first play during the 2007 Oxford Literary Festival. She is currently writing short stories and has had a poem published in the anthology 'People and Places'.

Jeni Bee's work was more like psychoanalysis, enabling her to study the human mind and resulting behaviour. What better basis for writing? Fiction it may be, but all fiction is based on human relationships and she has observed these at first hand.

Julie Adams is an escaped academic who now writes educational materials for OUP. In her spare time, apart from watching anything with Stephen Fry in it, she is working on a science fiction series for teenagers.

Liz Henderson enjoys writing fiction using an imaginative combination of her experience working in education and video-making. Passionate about trees she is now a dedicated volunteer for the Woodland Trust.

M.S.Clary, once a social worker, then an entrepreneur, now a writer. Published short stories in the 'Risky Shorts' and the 'Being John Black' collections. Currently working on a suspense novel set in the south of France and enjoying the research. In 2008 won the Deddington Short Story competition.

Margaret Wilcox enjoyed early success with her writing when her plays were performed in school concerts. As an adult, writing was often squeezed out by the demands of nursing training, bringing up a family and running an antiques business, but she published several articles in local newspapers and monthly glossies. Thinking about her lack of knowledge of her parents' life, and prompted by a grandson she started to write about her childhood, and has now revisited her first love, writing fiction.

Neil Hancox spent many years researching the properties and production of new materials. He finds that it is much more fun writing fiction – you can get the story to end the way you want, unless the characters take over!

Nicola Wilcox was first off the set reading list at infant school and has loved books ever since. She went on to art college but, nonetheless, became an advertising copywriter. A disorganised wife and mother, she joined the Turl Street Writers to create space in her week for writing. Life's still hectic, but the ideas keep coming. Nicola won a prize for the cover photo of *Turl Street Tales* from the Marlow Photography Club.

Penny MacLeod started telling stories at boarding school. She has worked in banking, administration, and as a radio and TV presenter in Saudi Arabia. She now records material for Radio Cherwell and Listening Books. Travel, bringing up a family and life have inspired her to write. She is currently working on a screenplay.

Robin Courage loves sailing and writing, occasionally simultaneously. His poetry and prose reflect a varied life of travel experienced in the Army, banking and management consultancy. In 2007 he read several poems at the Oxford Fringe.

As well as writing short stories, **Val Watkins** enjoys writing plays suitable for radio. She especially enjoys thinking up short plays with funny punchlines.

Yvonne Hands has been happily married to an Oxford don for many, many years, providing material for her ongoing project which is a comic take on life as a North Oxford housewife. She has never had a liaison with an American airman but would consider reasonable offers.

Printed in the United Kingdom
by Lightning Source UK Ltd.
135512UK00001B/187/P